Bradley

ENGINES OF LIBERTY
REBEL HEART

Published 2014 by DreadPennies USA, via the CreateSpace platform.

Cover illustration by Carter Reid (www.thezombienation.com)
Interior illustrations by Graham Bradley

ISBN: 978-0692205303

Got inquiries? dreadpennies@gmail.com

As of 1 July 2016, this book is not registered with the Library of Congress. I reserve the right to change that as soon as I have the resources, and/or feel like doing so.

Printed in the good old United States of America.

REBEL HEART

ENGINES OF LIBERTY, BOOK 1

.   Graham Bradley   .

DreadPennies USA

For Schaara, who let me narrate some pretty bad writing during our

courtship, and still decided to marry me.

"The time is now near at hand, which must probably determine whether Americans are to be free men or slaves ...whether their houses and farms are to be pillaged and destroyed, and themselves consigned to a state of wretchedness from which no human efforts will deliver them."

-General George Washington

26 August, 1776

CALVIN ADLER

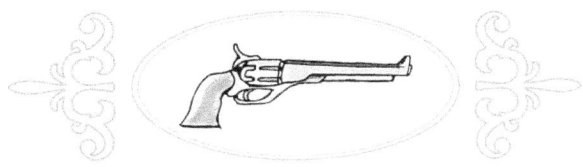

CHAPTER 1

Summer waned, but the late afternoon heat still slickened Calvin's forehead with gritty sweat. The pile of freshly sheered wool before him resisted his attempts to clean it, and a dull ache had built up in his back. His hands were numb, waterlogged from working all day, and yet the load never seemed to shrink. He cast a glance over his shoulder at the barn, where Mother and Father enjoyed the shade as they sheared even more wool off the flock. Calvin sighed, and hung his head.

Last year he had built a machine to speed things up—a sort of gin that would soak, scrub and work the wool until most of the oil and dirt were out of it, all with the crank of a single handle—but shortly after he'd gotten it working, the local mages had come by and cursed it with their wands. The contraption fell to pieces on the spot, its component parts refusing to connect ever again. They laughed as they walked away, indifferent to Calvin's plight.

When Father returned home later that day, Calvin complained about what they'd done. As usual, Father only capitulated to what the mages wanted. "You're lucky they didn't fine us! You shouldn't build things, Cal," he'd said in hushed tones.

"Why not?"

"Machines require special permits. There's a lot of paperwork and it's expensive."

"But why? It doesn't have to be."

"They're just dangerous, you understand?"

"No."

Father threw his hands up. "Look, things are a certain way for a reason. We can do it by hand without causing any trouble, so that's how you'll do it. No more questions!"

Every time Calvin asked why things *had* to be this way, that was usually the answer.

He resumed his work, wringing out a clump of wool and setting it in the clean pile to be dried. This year's yield was higher than last year's, and the Adlers were sure to fetch a higher price per measure; the material was always in demand, because the mages preferred it for their flying carpets and traveling cloaks.

Even if that fact drove the price up, Calvin didn't get why his family sold their wares to the mages. The lousy Brits always found a way to cut the final price by half. That rankled Calvin further: it meant he was working twice as hard as he had to for what they'd get paid.

Criminal. That's what it was. But when you didn't have magic, how to did you stand up to someone who did?

Mother and Father were thrilled at what higher sales meant for their prospects; they could perhaps pay off the flock and build their savings. Calvin didn't bother telling them they'd have been done two seasons ago if they'd just use some real equipment. His complaints would only fall on deaf ears. Scraping handfuls of wet, dirty wool against a washboard, Calvin longed for his machine, and seethed at the mages who had destroyed it. The echoes of their laughter still taunted him.

"Permits," he spat.

Using a thin rag wrapped around the back of his wrist, Calvin wiped his brow for the thousandth time. It was thoroughly soaked from the day's effort and now wholly ineffectual. He stood up and rested his back for a minute, craning his neck to survey the town in all its simple glory—log cabins and ramshackle farmhouses spotted the landscape. Thin wisps of smoke trailed up from cooking fires as housewives got supper underway. The people toiled, content for the most part, engulfed in their work. Overhead, a conspiracy of ravens swam lazily into the trees.

Calvin envied them, envied their power to spread their wings and just *leave* a place if they didn't like it. Nobody held them back, made them stay in the same spot, scrubbing dirty old sheep fibers until their fingernails stung, smiling the whole time like they enjoyed what they did.

Down the main road a trio of mages rounded the corner, their long red cloaks swaying behind them. Calvin froze, his eyes narrowing almost by reflex. The two older mages in front—Winston Fitznottingham and Hammond Birtwistle—had been tormenting the residents of Baltimore for most of his life. Calvin didn't know the third mage, who didn't look a day over fourteen years old, yet still wore the robes of a full officer. He walked behind the others with a profound kind of sulk that Calvin saw whenever he looked in the mirror—even when he was trying to hide it.

What bloody reason did a mage have to sulk?

Fitznottingham and Birtwistle were showing the new guy around town. The two elder mages drank their usual pungent ale from porcelain flagons, and when they'd drained the last of their cups, they used their wands to transfigure them into coins. These they placed in their pockets, careful to make sure a handful of the villagers were watching—in particular a young girl with pigtails staring up at them in wide-eyed wonder, despite her parents' pleas to keep walking.

"Bet that'd be nice to do, yeah?" Fitznottingham sneered at the girl, flipping the coin over in his hands. She nodded, eyes bright. Calvin saw fear on her father's face, even at this distance.

"Well, keep dreaming!" Fitz snapped. He flicked his wand at the girl's bare feet. Vines snaked up out of the ground and wrapped tightly around her ankles, holding her in place. The girl's eyes went from wonder to horror, and an awful shriek escaped her throat as

SHOWING THE NEW GUY AROUND

she kicked against the taut vines. Her mother begged her to be quiet and hold still so her father could work the vines off of her thrashing feet, but the girl would not endure reason. Still, the spell was ultimately harmless, if a little damaging to the girl's confidence.

Fitz and Birty strolled onward, chortling at their own wit.

Oh, what Calvin would do to them if he could get away with it. Sometimes he felt like people were right at the edge of their tolerance, and all they needed was the right push to fight back.

It wasn't completely unheard of; he'd seen it happen only once, a long time ago in Boston.

Calvin recalled the trip he'd taken with his father. They'd left Baltimore and led a horse-drawn wagon all the way up to Massachusetts, where Father knew of a captain who would deliver their wool to a wholesaler in Nouveau France, for a small commission. Their meager stock from that season had filled only a small part of the deck on the captain's ship; the rest of it was dried tea leaves in strong crates secured with a special kind of iron.

"*Frosted* iron," the captain whispered to Father. "So as it can't be magicked away by the mages, you see. It's a special product from Ohio. Your load's safe on this ship, Mr. Adler."

Father was impressed. "And all this tea?"

The captain told how he and a handful of his friends had planted the valuable crop many years prior, tended to it themselves, harvested the leaves and dried them with painstaking care. It would catch a king's ransom on the open market, compared to what the crew normally sold on their voyages.

Father and the captain shook hands and parted ways. Yet it would seem that not all of the captain's commercial associates had been so discreet that year. After Calvin and Father had gotten off the ship, a trio of mages showed up, wands in hand, and matching sneers on their faces.

At the time, Calvin hadn't understood what was happening. The mages demanded to know the captain's intent for the tea. He and his crew bristled at the question. Some of them quietly grabbed nearby instruments off the deck, but they weren't holding them the way they held tools. The captain stated his business, that they meant to sell their haul, and the mage casually said he'd have to confiscate the load.

"It just wouldn't be fair to the other colonists, who don't have any tea to sell," the mage had said, signaling for his companions to seize every crate of product. Calvin scratched his head at this; if the captain and his men had done all the work, why shouldn't they sell it?

Apparently the captain agreed with this sentiment. What happened next was burned into Calvin's memory sure as a branding iron marked livestock.

Some of the crewmen were still loading crates of tea leaves onto the deck of the boat. Half a dozen crates sat on a platform mounted to the dock, all rigged up with ropes and pulleys so it could swing out over the water. While the platform hung between the dock and the boat, the captain uttered a word in what sounded like an Indian language. One of the crewmembers, a bronze-skinned man with pitch-black hair shaved in an extreme pattern, drew a tomahawk from behind his belt, spun around and hurled it with stunning accuracy at the rigging. The tomahawk's blade bit into the ropes, sliced them clean through, and unlaced the complicated weave that allowed the platform to move. Six crates plunged into the salty water below, instantly ruined. To save the falling crates, the mages uttered summoning spells in the Old Saxon tongue, but the anti-magical iron did its job.

Calvin was pretty sure a fight had broken out after that, but he didn't get to see it. Father clapped a hand over Calvin's eyes and quickly whisked him away, telling him they were to return to Baltimore immediately.

Even now, Father refused to let Calvin speak of that day, and all of his questions since then had been met with a sharp command to put it out of his mind. Calvin had never forgotten it, though. After years of seeing Fitz and Birty squeeze coins out of the Baltimore residents, Calvin eventually understood why the captain had destroyed his load.

If he couldn't keep what was his, the mages sure as daylight weren't going to get it.

He kept that in mind as Fitznottingham, Birtwistle and their new charge strolled up to the Tanner house across the way, eyeing the wares in the front yard. Mr. and Mrs. Tanner were metal smiths by trade, and they guaranteed every tool they sold. For anyone else it would have been a risky business model, but Calvin knew the Tanners to be good people who made good instruments. At the moment there were three other men in the yard, talking with Mr. Tanner next to a row of newly made shovels.

"Right then, Tanner!" said Birtwistle, his British accent even more annoying through his drunken slur. "It's at time of the week again!"

Mr. Tanner went pale. His three guests exchanged a glance, then looked back and forth between Mr. Tanner and the mages.

"But, um, Mr. Birtwistle, it's only been five days, and—" Mr. Tanner began.

"They always get like this," Fitznottingham muttered to the new guy. "Trick is, you don't give 'em an inch. Watch old Birty here, he knows what's what."

"It's been two days since'a weekend, Tanner. 'At means it's a new week. Cough 'em up then, we ent got all day!" Birtwistle made a show of rubbing his thumb against his index finger. In his other hand he held his wand at his side.

Calvin's knuckles turned white around the wool in his hand. He could see it play out in his head now: Birtwistle would go about collecting like this two or three more times over the next couple of months, then make it the norm. Soon he'd be collecting twice a week. Then thrice. Then daily, and not just from Tanner. Everyone on the street would pay that way. Sure, the daily amount would be lower than the monthly amount, but not when you added it all up.

Calvin would protest to Father. Father wouldn't listen. Mother would go along with Father. Things would either stay the same or get worse. That was how it always went. Calvin hated how everyone just let it happen.

Tanner blanched and fumbled for an excuse while his customers backed away. Mrs. Tanner appeared in the doorway, face equally aghast. She muttered something to her husband about not having enough money yet from this week's business. Birtwistle clicked his tongue in disapproval, and the tip of his wand flicked nervously, like it was anxious to cast a spell.

Calvin found himself moving before he could give it a second thought. Mother and Father weren't right there to stop him, so...

He dropped the wool. In one hand he grabbed the handle of the sluice bucket, and with the other he snatched up a wooden rake that had been leaning against the wash bin. Hoisting the sluice bucket onto one shoulder, Calvin crossed the road in half a dozen steps and, holding his breath against the rapid-fire beat of his heart, called out to Mr. Tanner.

"Mr. Tanner! You still need me to water your grass?"

Fitznottingham flinched, not having heard Calvin approach from behind. The man's eyes were red and watery, refusing to focus the way a sober person's would. He was the perfect distance away.

Calvin pretended to trip. The bucket of disgusting water launched into the air and drenched Fitznottingham from head to waist, marring his fine robes with the grit and grease of several dozen sheep's worth of wool.

"You pikey little pillock!" Fitz shrieked.

"Oh! I'm sorry, Mr. Fitznottingham!" Calvin exclaimed. He'd

hung the rake over his shoulder when he'd "tripped." Gripping it tight, he spun around to face Fitz, allowing the end of the rake to catch a surprised Birtwistle hard on the cheek. The latter staggered back a step and immediately cupped a hand to his face.

If they hadn't been drunk, Calvin wouldn't have gotten within ten steps of them.

The third mage, the new one, jumped back wordlessly and avoided the whole mess. As Birty nursed his cheek, Fitz swore and lazily waved his wand, vanishing the water out of his clothing. He rose to his full height and leered down at Calvin.

"What then? The nerve of you, duffer trash!"

Calvin glared at the mage, rooted in place by a flaming batch of courage and a tiny garnish of fear. Had he really just done that?

"I'm mighty sorry, Mr. Fitznottingham! I keep my head low when you're about, as I should, and on account of payin' my respects I didn't quite keen to your proximity!" He rubbed a fair amount of his duffer accent on the words to sell the act.

"Why I never!" Fitz spat out a disgusting stream of blackened spittle. Some of the water had gotten in his mouth, then. "That was intentional!"

Mrs. Tanner looked dumbfounded, standing there in slack-jawed disbelief. Her three customers fixed Calvin with nearly identical looks of curiosity, but said nothing. It was Mr. Tanner who ran to Calvin's aide.

"Oh no, Mr. Fitznottingham! I saw the whole thing, the Adler boy dumps his bucket out in our yard to water the grass for us...

he tripped! Don't be angry with him, it was an accident!"

Fitz only spared Mr. Tanner the briefest of glances before jabbing Calvin in the ribs with his wand. "Accident or not, you're not paying proper heed to your betters!"

Calvin fought to keep his eyes from narrowing, fought to hold back the rage that boiled up inside him. As much as he wanted to tell Fitz to kindly go throw himself off a bridge, he held his tongue—if nothing else, Mr. Tanner had just put himself at great risk for Calvin. He wavered, mind racing for a way to shield the man from his actions.

"Again, terribly sorry, sir," Calvin managed. "Mr. Tanner's right of course, 'bout the grass and all. I was being clumsy and I dropped it on you ...and poor Mr. Birtwistle, well, he's got a good strong jaw an' such, really it's the rake that got the worse end of the exchange ..."

At the sound of his name, Birty grunted and clamored to his feet. "Do you think I'm stupid, you munter?"

I'd really love to answer that question. "Never, m'lord! You're a mage, after all! The rest of us is just duffers, you see? Myself, and the Tanners, and their three guests, and my parents across the road, and then there's the Parry family next door, and Mr. Parry wrestles down at the pub twice a week for prize money, he's on a win streak going two months if it's a week ...let's see, there's also the Martins, who push their handcarts all the live-long day, moving wares for us simple folk, and blast me if those carts don't get heavy 'round high noon, but those Martin boys just keep pushing. Of course, that's all we duffers do, is push and pull and lift and work with our hands while the sun's up, on account 'a we got no magic. Builds the body, I guess. If we had minds half as built as our shoulders, why, we wouldn't need you fine lords, now would we?" Calvin bit his lip for added effect. "So no, m'Lord Birtwistle, I'd never think you were stupid. Not a finer mage in Baltimore! Cept you, Lord Fitz. Call it even, then."

Birtwistle's eyes flitted around the open street as Calvin spoke, and something clicked in the back of his plastered brain: they were surrounded. The Parrys and the Martins and everyone who lived on their street had come out to see what the fuss was all about, and whether they intended to do anything or not, Birty could still do the math. Even with magic, their skills were outmatched.

Now it was on them to decide whether punishing Calvin for an accident was worth the fallout. *There goes your balance,* Calvin thought.

"I see what you're about, then," Birty whispered, his eyes steeling for a moment through the ale in his blood. "Clever one."

"I've been accused of worse things than wit, m'lord." Calvin had to fight every muscle in his face not to grin.

Birty's wand snapped into his hand. For the briefest fraction of a second, Calvin thought he was done for, that the mage might just be gutsy enough to mow down an entire neighborhood, and that it would be all his fault ...but then Birty trained the wand on Calvin's empty bucket that lay in the road.

"*Heofonfyr!*" He uttered the magical curse with exceptional relish.

The bucket split into pieces, which then hovered and spun in a tight circle, glowing hot like embers in a fire. The pieces rose up a few feet off the ground and blasted out in every direction. Parts of Mr. Tanner's yard caught fire, as did Calvin's and the Parrys'. A sheep bleated as far away as the Adlers' barn—a cry of pain, no doubt. Birtwistle cocked a half-smile, impressed with his work.

"Clumsy me," he sneered.

For added measure, Fitznottingham thrust his wand at the pile of wool in Calvin's yard and uttered a second spell.

"Formeltan!" The already-washed wool transfigured into a bubbling puddle of polluted tar, which pierced the evening air with a sharp stink.

"I do declare, it's just not our day, is it, Hammond?" Fitz asked his friend. "I swear I can't aim this thing to save my life." He cackled at his own joke, nudging the mage-in-training with his elbow. The trainee regarded them all sourly, like he was too good to be wasting his time with any of this.

A shrill cry filled the air, a cry Calvin knew all too well. It came from his family's barn, in his father's voice.

"Calvin! What the ...oh, Mr. Fitznottingham!"

There at the front door appeared Father, his clothes soiled from the day's labor. Mother came up behind him and took stock of the situation. Father rushed out into the street to fawn over Fitz's still-grimy robes; the water spell hadn't removed all the grit.

"Your idiot son dumped a bucket of filthy water on me!" Fitz said.

"I am so sorry, sir! We'll ...we'll..."

"Wash it all by hand," suggested the bored apprentice, folding his arms.

"Of course!" Father agreed. "And we can—"

"Save it, you nits," Birtwistle growled. He twirled his wand, muttered another spell, and removed the last of the water and oil from his friend's robes, good as new. "You forget who you're on with. That was a complicated bit of magic I just had to do, on account of your son. You reckon that ought to be free, then?"

"Surely not—," Mother began.

Fitznottingham cut her off. "Good. Glad that's settled." He struck out with his wand one more time and made a broad, sweeping gesture at the Adlers' land, muttering Saxon words under his breath. The very ground glowed with a dull, pulsing light, and for a brief moment Calvin feared that Fitz might burn their farm. Before a cry could escape his lips, the light pooled under a corner of the house foundation and then faded. With an evil grin, Fitz trained his wand at the window at that corner of the house— Mother and Father's bedroom.

"Pening fleon!" he said.

A sharp crack of splitting wood echoed through the house, followed by the unmistakable clang of crunched metal that could only be the family's strong box. Glass shattered as several pounds of gold crowns sprayed through the window, crushing it beyond all hope of repair. The coins slowed and drifted into the folds of

WILLIAM AND REBECCA ADLER

Fitznottingham's robes. From the look of it, Calvin guessed it to be most of what his family had saved for the past year.

Father gasped. Mother let out a muted whimper and raised a hand to her mouth.

"There. We'll call that settled ...for this month," Birtwistle sneered. "Right then! Fitz, Godfrey, this way. I think we've worked hard enough for one day."

As the mages retreated from the stone-silent street, pretending to be about a leisurely stroll, Calvin felt the heat of many eyes glaring at him, and not just from his parents. The Tanners, the Parrys and everyone else stared at him as if he'd just set fire to the general store.

Father cuffed him on the ear. "What the hell were you thinking, boy?"

"William, don't. Not in the street," Mother pleaded.

"Quiet, Becca." To Calvin, he said, "That was our share to repay the franchiser. It's due in a month and now we've got nothing. They'll repossess the flock when we can't pay!"

"How is that my fault? I've been sweating and bleeding into this mess just as much as you have," Calvin shot back.

"And now it's gone!" Father shouted.

"Why are you yelling at me? They're the ones who took it!" Calvin shouted back, pointing down the street at the mages, who might not have been out of earshot.

Father snatched his ear and twisted it, dragging him back to the house. Mother was right on their heels. Calvin grimaced all the way back into the house where Father threw him inside and barred the door behind Mother.

"Damn it all, Calvin! You've ruined everything! I told you not to cause problems, that there would be consequences. Now look at us! We'll never get that money back in time," Father said, tears forming in his eyes.

"Bet you we could if we used my gin," Calvin retorted. "You could have paid the franchiser a long time ago!"

"I hope you're happy, son. I hope your nerve keeps you warm next month when we're living in the woods and we're out of food. There you can build all the machines you want! You damn fool boy." Father trailed off and hunched over, his shoulders trembling as he sobbed, pressing the heels of his hands against his eyes. "Ruined. And we were so close."

Mother moved to Father's side to comfort him, not even looking in Calvin's direction. Calvin pursed his lips. He couldn't find it within himself to say anything more; it wasn't like his parents would listen.

He retreated to his room. He didn't doubt that he'd done a good thing, standing up to the mages in front of everyone else, and yet he hated seeing his parents in pain like that.

Yes, they were broke. No, it wasn't his fault.

Every day he hated the mages a little more.

*

Godfrey Norrington had remained as quiet as a mouse during the entire exchange between Fitznottingham, Birtwistle, and the young colonial duffer. The boy had very obviously attacked them on purpose, though he hid his intent with admirable skill. If there was one emotion Godfrey could detect without trying, it was anger.

As a full mage, he had a wide variety of magical aptitudes. Mancers were usually limited to just one skill—controlling an element, or communicating with animals, or some such. Mages, on the other hand, could always explore and enhance their natural talents. Godfrey had learned even before his tenth birthday that he could detect what he called the "red emotions." Lust, for example, was easily visible, and perhaps the most common. Jealousy was another (though people seemed to think it was green, for some foolish reason.) But nothing was ever more obvious than unbridled rage.

And that duffer brat, whoever he was, had been beet-red on the emotional spectrum when Godfrey first took notice of him. The sight of it gave him such a shock that he could only stare and watch the youth carry out his assault. Godfrey had never come across such a brazen duffer. Watching him explode on Fitz and Birty had given him the faintest taste of amusement.

Ever since Godfrey had been banished to the Maryland colony, he'd been starved for entertainment. So he'd let Birty and Fitz throw their tantrums and rob that family blind rather than execute the boy right there on the spot. Maybe if they hadn't been so smashed, they'd have seen the truth for themselves. Then again, not many mages cared to develop their emotilectural prowess. And that was fine with Godfrey; when it came to reading emotions, he liked being the best.

He glanced over his shoulder as they walked away, and watched the boy's father drag him back to the house. Godfrey thought of his own father far across the ocean in England, and for the briefest whisper of a moment, he felt for the young duffer.

My father's a complete prat as well, he imagined himself saying to the boy. The he squashed that thought. One didn't waste time making friends with duffers! He might as well befriend a diseased dog. Sighing to himself, Godfrey kept his hands clasped behind his back and brought up the rear behind Fitz and Birty as they marched back to the dormitory where they lived.

Godfrey had his own machinations upon which to dwell—

namely, how to get off this wretched continent and get back to England. Godfrey Norrington was meant for greater things than this, no matter what his git father had to say about it.

*

Around midnight Calvin awoke to a tapping sound against his bedroom window. Pushing himself up on the sawdust mattress, he groaned at the soreness in his body and sat upright to see what the ruckus was. He bumped into someone in the dark and froze. A cry formed in his throat, but it died on his lips, smothered by a gloved hand. Two more unseen hands pinned his arms to his sides. His body flooded with strength born of sudden panic. Calvin thrashed and tried to pull free, but the intruders had been ready for this, and they held fast.

"Hush now, Calvin Adler. We're not mages, and we're on your

side," whispered a voice beside his ear.

Against the dimly lit window he saw the silhouette of a third figure pulling the window closed. That was the tapping he'd heard—strangers entering his house!

"I am going to release you now. If you make any noise, if you call to your parents, we will subdue you with greater force. You will not enjoy it," the voice warned. "Understood?"

Breathing in short bursts through his nose, Calvin mumbled his consent. The glove pulled away from his mouth. He tugged free and staggered back, wishing desperately for a light, and even more so for a weapon. His first wish was granted: the man who'd spoken lit a candle, throwing up a circus of flickering shadows around the small room. Calvin narrowed his eyes.

"Hey! You were in the Tanners' yard—"

Immediately the hand covered his mouth again.

"Too loud! Be quieter. Last warning," the man said. Eyes wide, Calvin nodded, and the man relaxed, the candlelight flickering against the hard features of his face. His comrades flanked him, and Calvin got a good look at their faces.

They were of a large build and grizzled in appearance, what with their traveling coats, their high boots and all manner of gear about them. The leader—that was how Calvin perceived him—had a three-day beard and dark hair that hung in his eyes. The man on his left had sandy blond hair that curled, and the third man bore a prominent moustache that almost covered his lip.

Calvin took a deep breath and lowered his voice. "What are

you doing in my house?" he demanded.

"Won't be yours for much longer, the way I hear it. Unless of course someone were to return these." The leader dropped a small canvas bag at Calvin's feet. It thudded heavily against the floorboards. Whatever was inside, it clinked like metal. Calvin's heart beat a little bit faster.

"No way."

"Gold crowns. Every last one of them."

"Who are you?" Calvin asked.

"My name is John Penn. These are my associates, Griff Cade and Daniel Aberforth. We are, well, equalizers, of a sort," John said. "Some people need jobs done, and we bring in the tools to do them." He nudged the bag of coins with the toe of one boot.

"You lifted this off of Fitz and Birty?"

"Yeah. It was fun," said Daniel, the curly-haired man.

"No way," Calvin whispered. "How? They're mages."

"And we're technomancers," said John.

Calvin fixed the man with a blank stare. "Say again?"

"Technomancers," echoed the one called Griff.

"You're magicians, then?"

They laughed quietly. "No," John said. "It's science, not magic. Whereas pyromancers use fire or somnomancers manipulate dreams, technomancers use technology."

When John figured that Calvin didn't know that last word, he explained further: "Machines. Instruments. Things that can level the playing field against magic." He produced a printed square of

EQUALIZERS, OF A SORT.

paper from his breast pocket and handed it over. Calvin held it up to the light.

There was a drawing on the face of it, depicting a man in sturdy clothing, brandishing weapons at a man opposite him. This second figure was clearly a British mage, who held up his hands in an act of pleading. The inscription around the drawing read, "You can do any job with the right tool."

EVEN MAGES BLEED

"By the Crown," Calvin breathed. "You're rebels!"

The mustachioed man chuckled. "If only that began to cover it, kid."

"But you can fight mages?"

"All the time. Fight 'em, kill 'em, whatever it takes."

Calvin studied the drawing. The man on the left—a technomancer—brandished a knife and something else. Something Calvin had seen only in drawings, something that had been forbidden since time immemorial.

A handgun.

"No way. *No way*. You guys don't have guns. Nobody does."

The words hadn't even made it all the way out of his mouth before each man's hand was at his hip, digging in a leather holster and snapping a pistol out for proof. Calvin gasped; he reached out to touch John's gun, but John drew it back and replaced it in his holster, his fingers easily accustomed to holding and twirling the thing.

"This isn't a social call. We came to this town in search of new cadets. Mr. Tanner's skill as a metalsmith caught my eye, but somehow I don't think he has the temperament to do what we do. You, on the other hand ...what are you, about fifteen?"

"Yes, this summer past," Calvin answered automatically, eyes still fixed on the men's guns. *Real guns*.

"Good. You're older than a lot of kids we've had in the past," said John. "You want to learn how to shoot a gun?"

He couldn't believe his ears. "You serious?"

"Dead serious. And guns are only the simplest of our machines. You know how the mages have monsters that they control with magic? Well we have monstrosities of our own, made of metal and powered by engines. Tanner mentioned that you built a machine last year. It must have worked rather well for the mages to destroy it."

"It worked great," Calvin growled.

"Mechanical inclination will serve you well as a technomancer. There is no shortage of weapons and tools at our disposal, Calvin. What we need are good people to wield them. Our training camp is a few days away from here, and the director will accept new recruits for the next little while." John pointed a finger at Calvin, completing the thought.

"I ..." Calvin closed his eyes and rubbed the heels of his hands against them. "Hang on. You want me to leave my home and go train with guns so I can fight mages. Right?"

"Guns are better than sluice buckets," Daniel pointed out.

Calvin looked past them at his bedroom door. Beyond it was the short hallway to his parents' room. Their floorboards were still torn up from the mages' summoning spell, and it would be months before they could afford to have Mr. Tanner fix the strong box—unless they spent the coins at Calvin's feet. "I can't do that. I've already caused my parents enough trouble."

"More trouble than the mages?" John asked, arching one eyebrow.

Calvin's heart beat a little faster. "That's not it. I can't leave the farm. There's work."

"And workers here to do it. The farm will still be here in six weeks, especially now that your family's finances are secured."

Fidgeting, he frowned at the recruiters. "What's in six weeks?"

Daniel and Griff exchanged a hesitant look, but John never took his eyes off Calvin. "In six weeks there will be a massive, organized attack against the mages' greatest weakness on this continent. They don't know that we know where to strike them, which gives us the advantage. Our disadvantage is that we're hindered by our lack of numbers: we have more weapons than warriors. If you really want to save your town, if you really want to be rid of Fitz and Birty, then leave with us and become a technomancer. You'll have food, clothing, and your own equipment. In a matter of months, you and everyone you know and love could be free people. For that, the wool can run thin for a season, don't you agree?" John asked.

Calvin grew quiet, succumbing to a kind of stillness that was altogether alien to him. How many times had he dreamed of having power over Fitznottingham and Birtwistle? Surely he'd wanted it when he picked up his bucket and crossed the road. Well, here was his chance at last. What we he so scared of? Abandoning Mother and Father?

You can do any job with the right tool.

"What if I say no?" Calvin asked flatly.

John shrugged and let his hand fall to the gun at his hip. "Well, I did just spill a very sensitive secret. We protect our secrets, Calvin. There's a reason why you haven't heard of us."

Calvin glared at him. "You're kidnapping me? That's not really giving me a choice."

"Perhaps not, but I doubt that in your heart of hearts you want to stay here and keep cleaning wool so the mages can have cheap carpets. Think ahead to the next time Fitz and Birty come by to collect. How are you going to feel, knowing you could have done something to beat them?"

That Boston sailor appeared again in Calvin's memory, an everyday man who kept his hatchet-throwing skills a secret. Calvin thought of him hurling that tomahawk at the tea crane, sending months of his own hard labor into the sea with a single blow. He'd destroyed the results of so much work when he could no longer control it, when he wasn't living on his own terms.

Deep down, Calvin knew he was in the same position. While

the thought of running out on his folks made him a little sick inside ...the allure of being more powerful than mages, of not having to play dumb around them, was too much temptation to resist. If he joined this army and they could somehow teach him to make the mages' gifts irrelevant, wouldn't that be better?

"How long does the training take?" Calvin asked.

"Three, maybe four weeks. Then you start to see action," said Daniel, brushing a curled lock of hair off his forehead. "You show them you can work hard, maybe they'll even send you back to Baltimore when we strike. You can be part of the brigade that whips your local mages."

John studied him with eyes that made Calvin feel like an open book. "You have the hunger, kid. It's a hunger we all know. We've lost property and loved ones to the mages too, and we each doubted we could make a difference. Do yourself a favor and make the choice; there's nothing left here for you if you keep going the way you have, the way your parents have, the way all your ancestors have for centuries. Are you going to make a better life for yourself, or are you just going to roll over and take it like your old man?"

Calvin's neck bristled. He took a long, hard look at his shabby room, his forlorn bed, and the sack of gold coins at his feet. Three weeks to train, six weeks to attack?

A month and a half away from a lifetime of freedom? What was there to contemplate, really? He knew the answer.

"I'll do it."

~

GENERAL GEORGE WASHINGTON

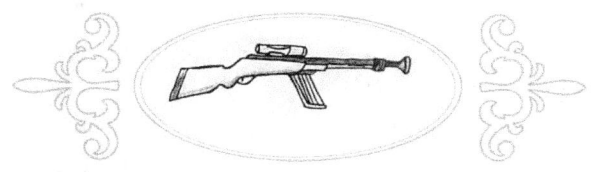

CHAPTER 2

Two days later, John announced that they had arrived.

Calvin dragged his exhausted body from the saddle where he'd sat for countless hours. The trip out of Baltimore had been quick and somewhat frightening; for all their talk about machines, the technomancer trio had come to town on horseback and expected Calvin to leave with them the same way. He'd ridden bareback all of twice in his lifetime, and both times the experience had left him sore in a very sensitive place.

Once out of town, they had gone to one of the seaports where duffers—non-magicals, like himself and the technomancers— docked their ships. Calvin expected they'd be travelling the rest of the way by sail.

36

He was half right.

This was when the technomancers revealed their machine. Something akin to a boat rose up out of the water, *from underneath the surface,* like a giant metal fish. Calvin just stared at it in the dim moonlight, wide-eyed and unbelieving. The vessel was in the shape of a large shark, and altogether larger than his house. A circular door opened on top and Griff led Calvin across a hastily laid gangplank, then directed him to climb a ladder down the hatch.

Down. Into the shark.

"We can travel this way, unseen, unheard, for miles," John explained once they were below. Calvin nodded, unable to conjure a verbal response.

The charm of the experience soon wore off, though. It took them two days to reach their destination. They picked up more recruits along the way, and during that whole period Calvin never once left the shark. For one who worked outside every day, it soon bothered him.

At least the new recruits were good company. Most of them were about his age, and congregated with Calvin at the rear of the passenger compartment, while the others huddled at the front. The first was Rusty, a twelve year-old girl with thick red hair. Her father had run a smuggling chain for the technomancers, only to be found and punished by the mages. Itching for revenge, she had run away with Stitch, a dark-haired middle son of a servant family who'd worked for Rusty's parents. Rusty's dress had once been nice, but a short life of flight had left it soiled. Stitch's clothes looked even worse, like they'd always been torn and repeatedly patched. Despite their appearance, their spirits were high.

There was also a tall, pretty girl named Lyla, the daughter of a tobacco farmer; an awkward boy called Cohen, whose family owned a bitumen refinery (one of the few mechanical trades approved by the Crown); and Avery, a rugged orphan boy who'd lived mostly in the woods and was rather adept with a bow. A sixth young man boarded early on the second day, with black hair and expensive clothes, but Calvin never got his name, as he had taken to conversing with the adults.

THE YOUNG RECRUITS

Each of them had a story like his own—the recruiters had seen them stand up to the mages, or utter something defiant, and then they were on route to this vessel, and now...

"Where are we?" Calvin asked, walking across the gangplank

on shaky legs, back toward land. Again it was dark, and he could only see the shark vessel's outline against the moonlit river.

"Virginia," Griff said. "Place called Mount Vernon."

"Are you serious?" said Stitch, wide-eyed.

"You've heard of it then?"

"Of course I have! This is where—"

"Ah, don't spoil it now. Y'all are about to go through orientation." Griff herded them down the dock, across a grassy field and around a row of smelly stables. There came into Calvin's view the largest mansion he'd ever seen, impressive even at night.

"Wow," he whispered.

"Are we staying here?" asked Cohen, scratching at his mop of straw-colored hair.

"You're staying in the barns. Pick it up now," John said, joining Griff.

"This is your house?" Stitch asked.

John shook his head. "This estate is in the custody of our Commodore, Mister McCracken. He's a colonial like us, and a technomancer, but he's paid up with the right people in the British nobility. They leave him alone, and the grounds aren't frequently searched. There are other protections in place as well." He didn't elaborate. Before Calvin could ask, Griff opened a door on the east side of the mansion and herded them inside.

Calvin was sandwiched between Stitch and Rusty, who both needed a bath real bad. But he only noticed that for a second; once inside the mansion, he could only stare in awe at the surrounding regality.

The walls were smooth, painted white, adorned with framed paintings and ornate decorations. Sconces held scented candles on the wall, filling the air with a light perfumed smell like vanilla and spice. The rug was a muddy brown, made dirty by thousands of footsteps. Calvin instantly wanted to roll up the rug, take it outside, and beat it with every ounce of skill and experience in him; such a dirty thing did not belong in a place so fine as this.

John Penn led them down a hallway to an open foyer, where a set of double doors stood open. Beyond that was a large semicircular room furnished with dozens of velvet purple seats, like an opera house—Calvin had seen pictures of one in a book before, one of the few books that the mages had allowed in the library at school. On the stage was a podium, and behind it stood a man.

"Take your seats. Orientation is about to begin," Griff said. He ushered them into the auditorium and closed the doors. Calvin looked around, took the nearest open seat and dropped down into it. It was soft, softer even than his bed at home.

What did Mother and Father think when they woke up, and I was gone, and the gold had been returned? His palms itched just thinking about it. Suddenly he wanted orientation done with. Get to the training, get to the good stuff, *get this done.*

The room was mostly filled by other recruits, whom Calvin presumed had come to Mount Vernon by other means. Some were rather old. Some were better-dressed than he, and others hadn't bathed in weeks. Men, women, boys, girls, their skin a variety of colors, some marred with tattoos and others with scars. Calvin counted thirty-three in all.

"Good evening," said the man at the podium, a gentleman of fine clothing and proper grooming. He was older, perhaps fifty, with graying hair and a well-trimmed beard, and large spectacles. He walked with a cane that he had leaned against the podium prior to addressing them. "I am Commodore Jonathan McCracken. The recruiters will have told you about us and our purpose. Newcomers almost always have the same questions, which we will answer here with a brief presentation. Pay attention to what you are about to see."

Without another word, McCracken took up his cane and strode off the stage. The podium descended into the floor and the lights in the room dimmed. Calvin craned his neck to see the source of the light, but couldn't get eyes on it. From off to his right, the smell of seasoned meat wafted over, and his stomach growled—somewhere in the mansion, supper was on the fire. This house held far too many wonders to focus on just one.

The curtain at the back of the stage split down the middle, and the two halves pulled aside to reveal a perfectly white sheet the size of the whole wall. Something clicked behind Calvin, then rattled, and then the most wonderful thing happened: moving images appeared on the sheet. *Moving images!* There was no other way to describe it. A voice filled the auditorium, narrating the show.

"The year was seventeen hundred and seventy-six, the tercentennial anniversary of the founding of Nova Britannia. The continent was enduring one of its harshest winters. Both the duffers and the mages alike fell victim to it, though the duffers were accustomed to such hardships. Then, as now, our forebears lived under the thumbs of magic-bearing oppressors."

Calvin heard murmurs and grumbles all around him. Everyone focused more intently on the pictures, which showed farmers working in the snow, trying to find wood to burn while the mages freely raided their storehouses to support themselves.

The narration continued. "One man decided he had had enough. He lit a new fire, not in the hearth, but in the hearts and minds of men and women all throughout Nova Britannia. This fire gained momentum, fueled by the dreams of many brave souls. Soon, hundreds and thousands of good people armed themselves with whatever they could find, and they marched on the mages' strongholds. Though this volunteer army was short on training and had no proper equipment, they dealt a series of humiliating defeats to their mage overlords, who had grown fat and complacent in their power."

The moving images stopped, replaced by a clicking slideshow of regular pictographs that showed towns on fire, mages overrun by angry ranchers with pitchforks, and men pushing large wheeled machines that hurled giant arrows like a sideways bow.

"The leader of this army was a ragtag ruffian named George Washington. At first nobody thought he could do it—they thought the mages were too strong, too many in number to defeat. He proved everyone wrong, and with every victory he added more to his army. George Washington was bold, cunning, intelligent, and, many say, possessed of extreme luck."

The moving images came back. A large man whom Calvin assumed to be Washington came galloping past on a horse, a smoking battlefield behind him. He stopped and dismounted; three men ran to his aid, poking and prodding at him, but Washington just waved them off. He showed them his coat and breeches, which were perforated by no less than eight holes. Calvin recognized the star-shaped burns as the mark of a mage's curse on wool. Though Washington's clothes were riddled with holes, he didn't have a single scorch on his body.

"No way," Calvin murmured.

"Before long, Washington had raised a formidable armed force. That was when the Crown realized what a daring opponent resided on the new continent."

Another pictograph popped up, a grotesque image of the King of Britain, drawn as an ogre with a crown. Calvin laughed. So did a few others.

"The King did not like this rebel at all. George Washington had made a fool of him and his mages. By way of retaliation, he not only sent additional war wizards, but he employed a new tactic as well: the King learned about the citizens, learned about life here in the colonies, and learned how to stoke turmoil amongst us. Books, leaflets, and slanderous print circulated among the duffers like candy."

Calvin watched an array of printed materials piling up on the screen. The headlines were sensational and offensive. They accused Washington of sacrificing soldiers for petty missions, gleefully leading his troops to slaughter, wasting the sacrifice of his would-be countrymen. Calvin narrowed his eyes. It was just like those rotten mages to smear the good name of a man who stood against them. A cowardly tactic by any measure. Washington couldn't fight the mages and his own people, too.

THE KING ACROSS THE OCEAN

"People began to turn their hearts away from the nobility of the effort. By the end, the word caused even more damage than the wand, and all the fantastic luck couldn't save Washington from being executed in a public spectacle."

A new pictograph swept by, this one of Washington bound in chains, standing between a trice of dragons. One bore the flag of England on its back, one bore Scotland's, and the third represented Wales. The pictograph shifted, and all three dragons doused Washington in flames.

"Rotten pox-marked inbreds," Stitch muttered.

"You said it," Calvin breathed. "Why have we never heard of this?"

"Long time ago," said Stitch. He mumbled something inaudible, counting on his fingers. "The year is nineteen hundred and ...eighty-four? So this was more than two centuries ago."

Calvin had already figured that out. It seemed Stitch was a little slow with numbers.

The lights came back on. Calvin feared for a moment that their talking had cut the presentation short, but then the podium rose again from the stage and McCracken reassumed his place behind it. The images kept appearing on screen.

"You have probably never heard this story," McCracken said. "The mages know what it would stir up in you if you did—that the loss of this hero would affect you these hundreds of years after his martyrdom. Well, we mean to seize on the passion of Father George and finish his work. In order to do that, we have to be braver, bolder, and above all, more powerful than his army in his day. That's where you come in."

MOVING IMAGES APPEARED ON THE SHEET...

Calvin leaned forward to get an even better look at the new pictographs as they appeared. This one was similar to the drawing on the card that John Penn had carried with him: a mage stood with his wand out as if uttering a curse.

Opposite him was a man in boots and breeches, overcoat and gloves. He had weapons strapped to every limb, a pistol in one hand and a knife in the other. He donned a leather cap and a pair of goggles as well as a look of sheer defiance on his face. A technomancer!

The pictographs clicked away, replaced by drawings of mages on brooms and carpets, running away from a technomancer on a strange-looking gryphon—at least it had the appearance of a gryphon, yet it was also very obviously a machine of some sort. A third image showed a troll cowering under the heavy fists of a clockwork giant.

"Make no mistake," said McCracken. "We intend to incite rebellion, and we have the means to hold an advantage over the mages. You will all receive training in superior weaponry, equipment, tactics, and strategy. Prepare to be tired, but take heart in knowing you will no longer go hungry."

The shifting images disappeared and the screen retracted into the ceiling, revealing long banquet tables behind McCracken. Fruits and vegetables, blocks of cheese, sizzling meats, heaping bowls of potatoes and bread rolls, crystal goblets with colorful liquids, and three huge turkeys …Calvin had never seen so much food before in his life. His stomach did a little somersault and his mouth watered something fierce. So this was what he had smelled!

"We stole this from one of His Majesty's sustenance farms days ago. By next week you will all be raiding farms just like it," McCracken said with a grin. "Come fill your bellies. Tomorrow the work begins."

Everyone moved at once. Each recruit surged toward the tables, taking the first open chair they could get their hands on. McCracken stood back, smiling proudly, encouraging them to carefully pack down as much as they could.

Calvin ate until his stomach ached. Hours later the recruits extricated themselves from the table, thanking Commodore McCracken for his generosity before following John Penn out to the dormitories where they would sleep. He only nodded as the recruiters explained that they'd be issued new fatigues and footwear tomorrow, and would be fine in the meantime.

From there the cadets were mostly sorted by age, then by gender, and Calvin ended up in a barracks with the five other youths from the shark. He only kicked off his shoes before plopping down onto a bed and falling asleep in his clothes, feeling fuller and happier than he had in his whole life. A new optimism welled up within him, bringing with it a sense of invincibility.

Then the morning came.

~

COMMODORE JONATHAN MCCRACKEN

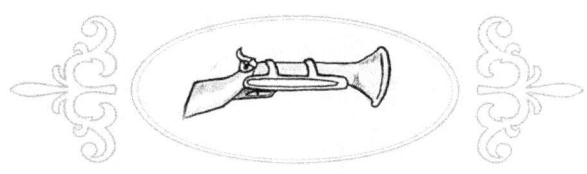

CHAPTER 3

A booming voice and a frigid shock tore them all from their slumber.

"Rise and shine, kiddies!"

Calvin shrieked as a torrent of ice-cold water dropped onto his bed. Gasping and sputtering, he jolted up and tumbled to the floor, landing hard on his elbows and knees. In his fright, his stomach lurched and he tossed up half of last night's dinner. A sharp stench told him that he wasn't the only one; the others had overdone it as well, and were paying for it.

"See, Peter? I told you there's always some that can't hold it in," said a boy towering over Calvin.

"I shouldn't have doubted you, Brian."

Calvin's heart thudded in time with his chattering teeth as he stood up to face Brian and Peter. Peter was a head taller than Brian, and looked to be maybe nineteen or twenty, while Brian couldn't have been much older than Calvin. The two boys—brothers, and sons of Mr. McCracken—went from bunk to bunk, emptying buckets on the recruits. Half of them were already up. Calvin wiped the water and slime from his face.

"What the hell?" he demanded. The younger brother, Brian, spun and hurled an empty bucket at Calvin. It smacked into his chest and left a stinging rebuke on his chilled skin. Calvin rubbed at the spot, wincing.

"There ain't no what-the-hells in here, my friend! Outbursts are something you earn. Get outside, greenie," Brian said.

"My shoes," Calvin protested, and reached down to grab them from where he'd left them last night. In two steps, Brian intercepted Calvin and shoved him toward the door.

"If you weren't battle-ready at bedtime, tough nuggets. Go!"

Within a minute, all six recruits were outside, most of them barefoot but for socks. Some had even stripped to their skivvies for the night, and it seemed that Peter and Brian would work them regardless of this fact. The adults from the other barracks were already there; it looked like they'd gotten a similarly rude awakening.

They started with distance runs. Peter and Brian ran in front of and behind the pack of recruits, prodding them along with sharp sticks and sharper words as they jogged for miles through the forest around Mount Vernon. Calvin soon learned not to complain when a rock or twig stabbed him in the foot, because it only earned him a swat and a warning from the McCracken boys. Instead he did his best to pick a clean path while still keeping pace—no easy task. Though the run beat up on his lungs after the previous night's indulgence, his body handled it well enough otherwise; he'd spent a lot of time on the farm chasing errant sheep.

Or at least, he used to.

After a six mile loop, they came back to the grounds. The McCrackens let them rest for all of five minutes before they made the recruits move heavy logs from one end of the stables to the other, in pairs. Calvin and the girl named Rusty worked together at first; she was deceptively strong for her size. They moved three logs each, and by the time he was done, his shoulders and back were burning real bad. But then they had to move fuel drums— some full, some not—and eventually they progressed to heavy pieces of machinery that he couldn't identify.

Some of the older recruits grumbled about taking orders from kids, and Calvin saw more than one surreptitious glare aimed at the McCrackens when they weren't looking.

Lunchtime rolled around. Mr. McCracken came to the stables with his kitchen staff, describing the meal in detail. Calvin's mouth watered again, though some recruits looked sick at the mention of food. An older man seemed as if he might pass out.

"Oh, sorry Pops," said Brian, fixing the recruits with a wicked leer. "They haven't done their swim yet."

"Silly me," McCracken said. Calvin got the impression that they'd planned this bit.

Peter and Brian kept the pressure on Calvin and the others, driving them down to the river that cut through the land near Mount Vernon. With no further preamble, they shoved the recruits into the water and ordered them to swim down the bank for a mile. The only mercy they received came in the form of an order to stay close to shore, lest they drown. Calvin was not very good at swimming, and it took him several false starts before he struck up a half-decent rhythm.

"Just breathe on every third stroke," said a boy his age as he swam past Calvin, cutting effortlessly through the water. "It's easy."

Calvin started to say "thank you," but the boy kept talking.

"And turn your head skyward, then make sure your lips are out of the water before you open your mouth. That's why you're choking." He sped off, graceful as a fish.

"I'm not choking," Calvin protested. But the boy was already gone.

If his manners had been lacking, his advice had not; Calvin's technique improved drastically. An hour later he made it down to where Peter McCracken stood. Calvin could barely pull himself onto the shore, his limbs were so weak.

"Where's your brother?" asked Lyla, one of the first to finish the mile.

"He had to rescue a recruit from drowning," Peter said. "Doesn't look like he's cut out for the physical side of this. He's been lagging all day."

"Will he be alright?" asked the boy called Cohen.

"He'd better be, or he's walking home," Peter said nonchalantly.

Calvin frowned at the sound of that, unable to do anything but breathe.

Lunch was lighter fare than the previous night—mostly bread, a little dried meat and some fruit. They washed it down with a measure of milk, and plenty of water. Calvin was careful not to take in too much. His guts still hurt from the morning.

The McCracken boys led the recruits on a long march around the perimeter of Mount Vernon so that they knew the boundary of the grounds. Peter told them not to pass that boundary, because that was where their father's protection ended. If the mages sensed people moving about in the woods, it would draw undue attention to Mount Vernon. Calvin couldn't see very far into the woods anyhow—the trees were far too thick, like a living wall of green.

"Last exercise of the day, and then you can clean up," Brian said, halting their march next to a wooden pen than stank horrendously of pig filth. The very air had an oily texture.

"What's the exercise?" someone asked. It was the swimmer boy, standing tall with his arms folded in front of him, his chest sticking out just a little more than necessary.

"Run across this sty to the other side, there and back three times," Brian said.

"Shoot. Cakewalk," grunted a bearded man with a patch over one eye.

"Just mind the pigs." Peter pointed to the north end of the pig pen. Five heavy, hairy beasts wallowed in the mud and waste, some of them idly cutting their tusks together. It wasn't immediately clear whether they were boars or hogs.

Calvin exchanged a glance with Stitch at his left. His expression mirrored Calvin's thoughts.

It can't be so easy.

It wasn't.

Peter opened the gate and let the recruits in. Their feet sank into the disgusting muck, all the way up to their ankles. Almost instantly the pigs spooked and shook themselves free of the filth, rising up to their full height. The biggest one in the middle had to weigh at least five hundred pounds, and possessed the most frightening air about him, because he was the most still. He didn't huff and puff and squeal like the others. Calvin was about to speak when Brian withdrew something from a satchel hanging on a fence post. Whatever it was, he hurled it into the pen, right behind the pigs. A sharp *crack* filled the air, and the frightened animals stampeded straight at the recruits.

"GO!" Peter roared.

Calvin had negotiated a fast-moving flock of sheep, but a herd of five-hundred pound pork was something else.

About half of the recruits went for it when Peter told them to. The rest went after Brian set off a second explosive device behind them, when the pigs were almost too close to avoid. Driven by a killer instinct, the huge beasts targeted individual recruits, lunging with their powerful jaws, intending to gore a leg or snag an ankle. The exercise immediately disintegrated into chaos, what with Brian chucking explosives at random into the pen.

Calvin got away from the pigs on his first pass, and that was all he had after the day's labors. He kicked and leaped with every ounce of his remaining strength, his bowels threatening to release under the stress. Mud sucked at his tired legs, made him push two and three times as hard as usual just to take a single step, and more than once he had to drop onto all fours to roll out of the path of a charging swine. Somehow he made it to the other side, relieved to see most of the other recruits with him.

One by one, the recruits pushed through. By the time the first wave had gone once, Calvin was on his second try. The task seemed interminable—two steps forward, one step back, again and again—yet he managed to reach the other side for a second time, slapping one disgusting hand against the wooden fence.

"How 'bout this, huh?" asked the swimmer boy, panting, lathered with the effort.

"Forget this," Calvin gasped.

"I'm Edsel, by the way."

"Calvin." He recognized Edsel as the other youth who'd arrived in the shark mimic, but had attached himself to the older group of cadets.

"Come on, kid. One more go!" Edsel punched his shoulder and took off.

"We're the same age," Calvin muttered. He took a deep breath, steeled himself, and returned for a third run. When he touched the fence, he waited for the burning in his limbs to abate, and for the rest of the recruits to make it through, nursing bruises and injuries from where the pigs had kicked them or shoved them down.

"Come on!" Brian shouted, throwing yet another bomb. The pigs were losing steam, but not ferocity. When recruits came close enough to bite, the pigs lashed out with even greater fury.

"We can do this!" said Edsel. He ran. About half the recruits went with him, summoning the dregs of their strength to evade death by hog. Calvin looked covetously at the far side of the pen, prepared himself for a last run, and charged.

He was halfway through the stampede when a cry of agony stopped him in his tracks. He turned and saw an older man clutching at one leg. It was bent in a very incorrect direction, streaked with blood, and one of the pigs had halted to come back at him, its right tusk covered in dark red gore.

One of Brian's small explosives hit the pig right in the side of its neck. It caused no wound, but the sound and impact made the pig abandon the hunt temporarily. Peter McCracken grabbed a long pole that rested against the fence, and then jumped into the pen and rushed to the patch-eyed man with practiced skill. But rather than help the recruit to his feet, he crouched down and yelled in his face.

"How are you going to beat mages if you can't even beat a pig?"

"Please!" the man sobbed, rocking from side to side. Calvin couldn't take it. He ran back and hooked his arms under the man's shoulders, intending to pull him the rest of the way, but Peter whacked the back of Calvin's knee with the pole he carried— Calvin noticed it had a snare at the end—and told him to get away. Calvin stumbled into the muck.

"Hey!" Calvin snapped, getting back up. "What's your problem?"

"Get back to the fence!" Peter shouted angrily, even as a nasty-looking boar homed in on Calvin. Peter expertly looped the snare around its neck and yanked hard, pulling the hungry beast onto its side. Thus entangled in the snare, Peter again struck Calvin and told him to get gone.

Calvin lost it. He smacked Peter's cheek, leaving a streak of mud across his face. He drew back his hand to hit the McCracken boy again, but Peter was too quick; he dropped the pole and lashed out with his fists, hitting Calvin's elbow, armpit, ribs and jaw. A knee to the groin sent Calvin sprawling into the muck. Half his body was numb. The world faded, but before the lights went out, he thought that maybe, just maybe, being a wool merchant in Baltimore was better than this.

*

Calvin lay on the floor of the brig, a square room cut crudely from the earth beneath the mansion. It smelled of dirt and straw, and the air was moist. A layer of stinking, drying grime covered most of Calvin's body, and he found himself longing for one of the buckets of cold water that had woken him up that morning.

The door opened at the top of the stairs, and Jonathan McCra-

CALVIN COULDN'T TAKE IT...

-ken descended the steps.

"Calvin Adler, is it? On your feet."

Calvin got up, scowling in the dark.

"I trust you've learned your lesson about striking officers," said McCracken, peering through the bars from a safe distance.

"The officer was beating an injured man," Calvin protested.

"That doesn't matter. My sons know what they are doing," McCracken said, resting both hands on the pommel of his cane.

"His leg was broken! He'd been gored, and Peter took a club to him."

"Do you want to be a TechMan, or do you want to stay comfortable? What Peter did was no less merciful than what a mage would have inflicted upon that man on the battlefield. The purpose of these exercises is to build up your bodies and prepare your minds for the stress of combat against a superior foe. Today was easy. It will only get harder from here, cadet," McCracken warned.

"And what about that recruit? Will your boys beat him into running on a busted leg?" Calvin demanded.

"You don't get to talk to me this way, Adler. You're in enough trouble as it is."

Calvin balled his hands into fists to keep the tremble out of his voice. "My entire life, we've taken abuse from the mages. We've sat back and watched them do whatever they wanted because we couldn't do anything to stop them. John Penn brought me here because we're supposed to change all of that."

"John Penn brought you here because the TechMan army needs technomancers," Commodore McCracken said. "Any army is built on a command structure, and each member of that army will honor that structure."

"Your sons act like mages, Commodore. Are they going to act the same way when the attack is over? I thought we were fighting to beat the tyrants, not become them."

McCracken drew in a sharp breath and narrowed his eyes. "Choose your words carefully, boy. You say that again and you'll walk home."

His tone gave Calvin pause. Something in how he said it implied that he didn't literally mean *walk home*. McCracken picked up on his comprehension and smiled.

"Good. Now: I especially will not tolerate you comparing me or my sons, or any of the TechMans, to the British. You were due to be released in six hours, but I am increasing your punishment to twenty-four. And you will make up for the training you will miss in the interim, understand that."

Without waiting for a response, McCracken hobbled over to the stone stairs and negotiated his way to the door of the brig. Calvin watched him rap his knuckles against the iron slab, then give the password before it was pulled open from the other side. McCracken departed without another word, and the heavy door slammed shut, leaving Calvin alone in the deafening silence.

He was glad that it was dark. He wouldn't have wanted anyone to see him shed a tear over his situation. Cursing to himself, Calvin turned his thoughts to a few nights ago when John Penn's crew had broken into his home. He wished he'd have called out for his father. Too late for that now.

Then again, he didn't necessarily have to stay here ...

Calvin sat down and rubbed the pain from his sore legs, doing his best to stretch out the kinks. He would need healthy legs tomorrow.

Forget walking home. He would run, and damn anyone who tried to catch him. Calvin Adler was done with the technomancers.

~

AMELIA McCRACKEN

CHAPTER 4

Calvin didn't know what time it was when the brig door opened again. He'd prepared a litany of insults to sling at whichever McCracken man came down the stairs, though he stopped himself when he saw a girl with a tray of food.

"Good morning," she said, almost jovially. "I brought you something to eat."

"Thank you." Calvin's voice cracked, his throat dry from hours of thirst. The girl first passed a canteen through the bars, and he drank from it greedily.

"Not too fast or it'll come back up," she cautioned. "I'm sorry you're down here."

Calvin hesitated. She was downright kind. Her hair was braided in two short tails that hung behind her head, out of her way. Her clothing was clean, and she smelled ...pleasant. Judging by the look of her, she was also a McCracken. He said nothing, but accepted the food as she passed it to him—an apple, two rolls, and a slice of cheese. It might as well have been a king's feast, for how hungry he was.

"My name's Amelia," she went on.

"Calvin," he managed between bites.

"I heard what you did. Hitting my brother, I mean."

Calvin paused and considered the roll in his hand. "This ain't poison, is it?"

She actually giggled. "No. Knowing Peter, he probably deserved it."

Calvin stared at her, suddenly suspicious. Maybe Commodore McCracken was testing his penitence. "Did your father send you down here?"

He saw genuine honesty in her eyes. "Yes, but he told me not to talk to you. He's overseeing the other recruits this morning though, so he won't know. I snuck the cheese. You should try it, it's called *brie*. I'm pretty sure it's French."

Dipping a slice of the apple into the soft cheese, Calvin raised it to his mouth and nibbled at it. The taste was new to him— mostly he only ever ate cheese made from goat's milk. This new cheese mixed well with the fruit, and he craved more of it.

"Thank you," he said again. "I hope you're not going to get in

65

trouble."

"That would involve Dad paying attention to me, and he never has time. He's too busy building an army." Amelia waved him off, but he sensed a deeper bitterness behind her words. "So I'm curious: what made you do it?"

"Join the technomancers?"

"No, put a pig-crap handprint on Peter's cheek."

Calvin choked on a bite of the apple, trying not to laugh. Amelia giggled again, and he found he liked it when she did that.

"He hit a guy who had broken a leg. It was wrong, and I tried to stop him," he said.

Her eyes grew wide. "Wow. Don't let my dad tell you that you did the wrong thing, because you didn't. My brothers ...I mean, they're family and all, but they're prats sometimes. They're harder on you recruits than I think they have to be," Amelia said.

"Maybe it's for the better. They do have a point, that the mages won't go easy on us out there. Did they hit you when you did it?"

Amelia frowned, puzzled. "Did what?"

"All of the training stuff."

"Ha! I'd love to be a TechMan, but Dad won't let me. He doesn't want me anywhere near the fighting," she said bitterly. "I have to get by with watching you recruits from the windows. I pick up things here and there. I could tell you how to load and aim a rifle, but I've never gotten to fire one before."

"There are rifles here?" Calvin perked up. "I've only ever heard

THE OTHER MCCRACKEN

of those."

"Please, we have rotating guns and even cannons. If the Brit mages ever got it in their heads to storm this place, we'd cut down thousands of them. My Mom was a dead shot back in her day." When Calvin frowned at the expression, she explained, "She hardly ever missed."

"So your mother was a TechMan, but your father won't let you be one?"

Amelia nodded and looked away. "She died. In battle."

"I'm really sorry."

Amelia traced a finger down the bars of the brig and shrugged one shoulder, trying to hide the hurt. "She rode on a gryphon mimic, that's one of the two-man flying machines. They carry a pilot and a gunner, and she was the gunner. Her pilot was even Jack Badgett, can you believe that?"

"I've never heard of him," Calvin admitted.

"Oh, that's right. Guess that's the point, though. Badgett, he's a legend. He's taken out fifty mages in flight, another fifty on the ground, he's never been shot down, and he's never lost a gunner. Well, he hadn't anyway, until Mom went down a few years ago. A mage on a broomstick hit her in the neck with a curse, and it landed on a gap in her armor. She fell right off the gryphon. Badgett found her body in a swamp down the coast." Amelia sniffed. "Dad says it was a one-in-a-million shot. We never caught the mage who cast the curse."

"That's really awful." Calvin knew a pain in his chest, stirring up something deep inside him. He wanted to comfort her, though he had no idea what else to say.

Amelia shrugged again. "Dad made sure Badgett got demoted after that. He doesn't fly gryphons anymore, just little dragonling mimics. One-man machines, those." As if clearing her head, she blinked a few times and looked him in the eye. "Sorry, lost in thought there. I really should get going, I have other chores. Are you finished?"

Calvin looked down at the food tray. He'd eaten every scrap of it.

"Yeah. Thank you, again."

"Don't mention it—seriously, I'll get in trouble. You were only supposed to have bread and water. The extra food was for standing up to Peter," Amelia said, retrieving the canteen.

"My lips are sealed."

"It was nice to meet you, Calvin."

"And you, Amelia."

She gave him a gentle smile and retreated up the steps. A shiver ran down the back of his neck, and Calvin suddenly felt ten pounds lighter.

Maybe he wouldn't abandon Mount Vernon just yet.

*

Commodore McCracken was good for his word: Calvin had to make up the physical training that he'd missed while in the brig, all while still wearing the same filthy clothes from the day before. While Peter ran the main body of recruits, Brian cracked a whip on

Calvin and pushed him ahead, making him run faster and swim farther than the others. Calvin noticed that the broken-legged man was gone. Stitch said the McCracken brothers had sent him to "another facility" for treatment. Calvin hoped that the man was okay.

After the running, the lumber-moving (where he carried logs by himself), and the swimming, he had another stint in the swine run. Calvin fixed Peter with a withering glare, but said nothing when Brian shoved him into the stampede and barked at him to run it four, five, six times. Calvin made it, staggering through the muck at the end of the sixth run, winded like he had never been before. All of this done before lunch, and he finished in good time. The McCrackens walked him back to the stables where he cleaned up in a horse trough, then joined the other recruits in the dormitory for a quick lunch of bread, milk and jerky.

That afternoon they started learning firearms. Brian and Peter explained the basic principles of a handgun, including the parts, how to clean them and how to load "rounds" into the revolving "cylinder." Once they got that down, they learned how to load extra cylinders and clip them to their belts so that they could quickly replace a spent cylinder in combat. Calvin's nimble fingers moved across the bits and pieces quickly, as he was used to fishing out small burrs and other debris from sheep's wool. Stitch, Avery and Edsel were also pretty good at it. In fact, Edsel seemed to be good at pretty much everything.

When it came time for target practice, Calvin's accuracy was lacking. Edsel hit the target three-quarters of the time, and out of those shots he got pretty close to the center. Calvin only hit it half the time, putting him in the lower quarter of the rankings. Even Rusty was better at it than he was.

That changed the next day when Peter and Brian upgraded the recruits from pistols to rifles. The rifles took the same preloaded cylinders as the pistols, and while they could fire handgun rounds, they were especially effective with rifle rounds. Cleaning the longer weapons took more time, and they also took longer to line up and fire, but there could be no mistaking the advantage of a rifle over a pistol: a bullet flew straighter from the barrel of a rifle, over a greater distance.

Edsel may have been better with the handguns but Calvin topped him and sixteen other cadets with the rifles, practicing on dummies wrapped in red cloaks and mounted three hundred paces away. Calvin enjoyed the incredulous look on Edsel's face when he put five bullets through the target in a space no larger than a gold crown. Peter and Brian graded his performance, taking notes on sheets of paper that they kept hidden from the cadets. Calvin wondered what they said about him.

On the third day of firearms training, they upgraded to the heaviest gun of all: the blunderbuss. The tactics behind it were different from the handgun or the rifle. A blunderbuss was a weapon of sheer chaos. As Brian handed out cotton swabs for the recruits to plug their ears, Peter explained the new weapon to them.

"Flip this switch here. A hinge will expose the back of the

barrel. Pack in a charge, a fiber cloth and a handful of pellets. Tighten this clamp here, close the hinge, set the hammer and flip the safety off." Peter kept the barrel pointed skyward the whole time. Once everyone had their ears stopped with cotton, he turned the weapon on a wooden dummy and fired from the hip.

Flame and smoke spewed from the wide open mouth of the thick-looking shotgun. Instantly the dummy exploded in countless places, sending wooden splinters in all directions as multiple bean-sized pellets ripped into it with lethal force. Calvin's jaw hit the ground.

"Whoever survives a shot from the blunderbuss will wish he hadn't," Peter said flatly.

Calvin tried to imagine using the different guns in different scenarios. The rifle would be ideal for picking off mages at a distance, perhaps even from a concealed position. The handgun would be quicker, better at close quarters, though he needed to improve his accuracy. As for the blunderbuss ...that was less about shooting someone and more about making a statement. He couldn't even imagine a mage's shield spell repelling that much hot, fast-moving metal.

He and Stitch took turns loading, firing and cleaning the blunderbuss. By day's end the cadets had ruined better than ten wooden dummies, their bodies pumped full of lead and steel.

Night fell. The cadets had dinner, chatted quietly in the dormitory, and drifted off to sleep to recover some of the strength they'd given up during the day's exercises. Already it felt routine to

Calvin, though a mere four days had passed since training began. He slept, and dreamed of many things.

Fighting mages.

Mother and Father.

Amelia.

*

The bucket of cold water didn't shock him as badly on the fifth day. Like the others, Calvin had taken to sleeping in the fatigues that the McCrackens had issued, all the way down to his socks and boots. He rolled out of bed and darted outside to start running with the others. Six miles later they stopped, moved some heavy materials, took a mile swim and negotiated the swine run. Lathered in grime and sweating like a crook in court, Calvin dragged himself with his fellows to the stables, where Brian showed them how to handle and load clay-pot explosives

There was little technique to handheld grenades, even less than with the blunderbuss: pack it, light the fuse, and throw it away like a poisonous snake before it could take your hand off. Calvin learned that the biggest problem was throwing it at the right time; chuck it too early and the pot might hit the ground before it exploded, scattering its contents and wasting their potency.

"Each of you, pack four grenades. Load your pistols, divide up the rifles and the blunderbusses, and take three hours of R&R," Peter said. Calvin and Rusty, who had been packing grenades together, exchanged a confused look.

"We get the afternoon off?" asked Cohen, still sticking a fuse in his grenade.

"No, you're getting your evening hours ahead of schedule. Tonight we will raid an Imperial supply farm," Peter said. "Father told you that you would be doing so in a week, and this is that week."

Calvin instinctively looked to Stitch, who had already met his gaze, and he could tell they had the same question.

"A full-on, armed raid?" Stitch asked.

"Is there a problem, cadet?" Brian said.

Avery said, "Shouldn't we practice a little more?"

"You've been practicing non-stop for days. We're of the opinion that cadets hit a wall at that point, and a raid makes it a little more real. Helps you get to the next level. Plus, food doesn't exactly fall from the sky," Brian said.

"Check your gear, get your rest, and be ready in three hours. Dismissed," Peter said.

*

Calvin disembarked the shark submersible this time more steadily than he had when it first delivered him at Mount Vernon. With a blunderbuss in hand, he followed Brian's silent lead. Bringing up the rear were Avery, Stitch, Rusty, and Lyla. Peter would pilot the submersible farther down the river, depositing Edsel, Cohen, and another band of cadets, until they could spread out and hit the farm from multiple points.

There was no moon tonight. Brian said this was a twofold blessing: it would be harder for the mages to see the TechMans, and any mage or mancer with lunar magic would be at his weakest. This was especially true of faunamancers, who drew on the moon to control the moods of animals. Calvin was glad for any advantage. No matter what he'd learned in the last week, he'd never done anything like this. The closer they came, the faster his heart thudded in his chest.

He could still do this, right?

Stitch and Rusty dragged a four-wheeled handcart behind them, still dripping from the trip down the river. As the shark mimic was too limited on interior space, they had strapped it to the submersible's roof. Peter had parked the shark in reedy shallows, and in the effort to get the handcart on solid ground, it had fallen into the river, dislodging the axle on one side. Calvin couldn't help looking over his shoulder every time it squeaked or protested.

A British farm loomed a hundred yards away. As much as he wanted to have faith in the blunderbuss, a lifetime's experience with the mages couldn't be washed away after just five days of training. He wanted every angle covered.

"How many cows are we taking?" Calvin whispered to Brian.

"None; they'll serve another purpose. Look, up ahead at the mages' storehouse. We haven't hit this farm in over a year, so they won't expect us. Stitch, Rusty, take the cart over to the house. Avery and Lyla, provide cover for them. If you see a mage, *shoot*. Empty the cylinder—most of them wear shield spells, and it will take more than one shot," Brian said. "Calvin, you're with me. Move!"

They had scarcely taken five steps when a barrage of explosions perhaps a quarter-mile away lit up the pitch black night. Immediately there followed a thunder of hooves and a chorus of angry cattle.

"Damn, they're ahead of schedule," Brian said in a louder voice, abandoning all caution. "Rusty, Stitch, get going!" He plucked a grenade from his hip, lit the fuse with a flint switch, and hurled the bomb into the stampede. It rocked the ground and the herd steered away from the barn and ran for the sleeping quarters where the mages stayed.

Calvin kept his grip tight on the blunderbuss. His job was to protect Brian—if the cattle needed to be steered away from them, he could fire the blunderbuss faster than Brian could direct another grenade. Thirty seconds crawled by like an hour, and Calvin's eyes never left the windows of the mages' quarters, wondering when they would engage the technomancers.

"Hey!" Brian shouted, taking the blunderbuss and thrusting something into Calvin's hand. "Pay attention!"

"What?" Calvin asked. Brian had given him a large, sheathed knife, and was pointing over by the barn at Lyla, who had her hands cupped around her mouth.

"The door is locked with magic!" she shouted.

Stitch, Rusty and Avery were firing at the mages, who had started pouring out of their sleeping quarters, wands in hand.

"Stab the lock with that knife. Go!" Brian hurled another grenade, took up the blunderbuss and fired it over the cattle at the mages. Voices cried out in pain over the mooing livestock.

And then Calvin was running full-out toward Lyla, squinting in what weak light was cast from the farmhouse windows. A large metal padlock glinted on the door and he reached for it, but it swung to the side, evading his grip. Twice more he tried and failed, understanding what Lyla meant by *locked with magic*. He simply couldn't touch the thing. He unsheathed Brian's knife, aimed at the padlock and stabbed. This time it held perfectly still until the blade contacted it, and then it simply disappeared, an illusion destroyed by the touch of the knife.

Stunned, Calvin turned the knife over. "What's this thing made of?"

Lyla shouldered him aside and pried the doors apart. Stitch and Rusty pushed the cart inside, and they went about filling it with whatever they could grab. By the time they were pulling out, Brian had worked his way over to the barn. He tossed the spent blunderbuss to Calvin, who deftly reloaded it on the run as Brian and Avery covered their retreat. The mages were busy casting what weak spells they could conjure to keep the cows from plunging into the woods, lest they be picked off by bears or large predator cats.

Elsewhere on the grounds, red flares shot into the air, sizzling and fading after soaring to great heights. That was the retreat signal from Peter's group.

"To the shore! Move, move!" Brian brought up the rear. He was looking the other way when a mage on a flying carpet came up behind him, wand raised, a half-uttered curse on his lips. Brian

GET DOWN!

didn't see him, but Calvin did.

All conscious thought abandoned him. He had nothing inside but the urge to protect his comrade and deter his enemy. For this, there was only one thing he could do.

"Get down!" Calvin pointed the blunderbuss at the mage. Brian obediently ducked as Calvin darted forward, leaping over Brian's prostrate form. Squinting in anticipation of the flash, Calvin crushed the trigger.

In the split-second of muzzle flare he saw a look of fury and disbelief on the mage's face. The force of the blast took the mage off his feet as a handful of grapeshot ripped into his robes. Calvin felt, rather than heard, the man's heavy body hit the ground. The carpet lost all momentum and landed in a heap of stiff fibers.

All was still.

He had just taken out a mage.

Hands seized his arms, and he heard words through the sharp ringing in his ears—Brian was telling him to run, to get back to the mimic. Calvin ran, accustomed now to obeying the militant McCracken brother. The shock would catch up later.

For now, all he felt was the rush of victory, and he wondered how the first Revolution might have ended if George Washington's men had possessed weapons like this.

~

BRIAN McCRACKEN

CHAPTER 5

The weight of firing his blunderbuss directly into a mage would not leave Calvin's conscience anytime soon. He tried to remember all of the bad things that Fitznottingham and Birtwistle had done to his friends and family, but that didn't help. The mage Calvin shot was not Fitznottingham or Birtwistle. He was somebody Calvin did not know, and yet ...

Back at the dormitory, the recruits were bustling with tales of triumph, comparing stories with one another. Calvin quietly confided his concerns to Stitch, who'd already been through one traumatic plight on a farm.

"Yeah, it's a weighty thing, to know you've killed a man. I don't know what else you could have done, if he was going for Brian," Stitch said.

"It's not like it would have been some great loss," Calvin grumbled.

"One less McCracken, right?" Stitch said.

"Right," Calvin smiled. "Dime a dozen around here."

He wondered if Amelia had thought of him today.

*

If Brian McCracken felt any gratitude toward Calvin for dropping that mage, he had a funny way of showing it.

Training for that morning had been cut short after the swim session. Peter took the other recruits back to the stables to clean the equipment, but Brian put Calvin in charge of stocking the supplies they had stolen from the British farm. Not only was Rusty and Stitch's cart full, but two others besides, and the pantry where they stored their goods was meticulously organized.

"Keep it this way, everything straight and orderly," Brian said, after showing Calvin around. "Hop to it, kid."

We're the same age, Calvin thought, fuming. He ached to be outside with his fellow cadets. Instead he had to catalog grains and beans by weight, scribble the numbers into a ledger, and pack it all into cans. How this would help him fight the British Empire, he could not see. Part of him suspected that Brian was jealous of Calvin for hurting a mage, while all he'd done was throw bombs at cows. Maybe Brian wanted the other cadets to get better at technomancy than Calvin.

"Brian, I—oh."

Calvin nearly dropped a ten-pound can of dried corn on his toes. Amelia stood in the entryway to the pantry, her hair double-braided again, her skirt and blouse partially covered by an apron that was smudged from the day's work.

"Um, hello, Amelia," he said. His face felt hot.

"I didn't expect to see you here. Normally this part is Brian's job," Amelia said.

Calvin breathed in the soft vanilla scent that seemed to float off of Amelia's skin. Brian could dump his chores on Calvin anytime if it worked out this way.

"How've you been?" she asked, moving over to the scale and picking up the ledger where he'd left off. They easily fell into a working rhythm, as if they'd done this many times before.

"Busy," Calvin said, waving a hand at the food. "As you can see."

"This is a good haul. Could use some more meat, but that's easy to come by," she said. "I just had to clean out the inside of the shark mimic. Dirty job, that."

"Your dad won't let you study with the cadets, but he'll let you clean the mimics?" Calvin asked.

"He thinks it will keep me out of trouble." Amelia grinned and lowered her voice conspiratorially. "He doesn't know, but I have taken the shark out a couple of times. Just up and down the river."

"You can drive that thing?"

"Yes. It's so great! You're going to love piloting one. Oh, here." She handed him a canvas sack of apples. His hand brushed hers as he took it, and his ears burned. He wondered if this was how it went when a girl fancied you, or if she was just being friendly. He told himself not to overthink it—there were already enough ways to get in trouble with the McCrackens.

"Thanks," he said, putting the sack on the fruit shelf.

"So Brian has you doing his chores, huh? He must be afraid of you," Amelia said.

"Whoa, what?" Calvin halted and almost dropped a can.

"He's done this once or twice before—if there's a recruit he doesn't like, he'll put them on remedial duties for a day or two, just to slow them down. Makes them look worse on paper so they get grunt work assignments when it comes time to go into the field," Amelia said.

"That prat! Wait, so that means I'm good at all this?"

Amelia shrugged. "So far, yeah. But you guys haven't even started the good stuff. Next week, if you keep the schedule, you'll start mimic simulations."

"If I keep the schedule," Calvin muttered, stocking another can.

She lowered her voice. "Don't be in such a rush to hit the field. I've seen thousands of recruits graduate from training, but it's always the same people in charge who pass back through."

"You don't think they all die out there, do you?" Calvin asked.

"Well, no. I mean sure, some do, but mostly I meant ..." She looked down and bit her lip. Was he imagining the flush of red in her cheeks? "You're not in a rush to run off and get killed, are you Calvin?"

"Definitely not. I am here to run off and ..." he thought about saying *do some killing* but he didn't want to think of the mage again. "And fight for something worthwhile."

Amelia stopped writing in the ledger and rested her hands on the counter. "Why do you feel that way, Calvin?"

He pursed his lips as he recalled the tea merchant in Boston, telling Amelia a brief version of the story. "Before my dad could take me away from there, I asked a man in the crowd what was going on. I wondered why the captain had thrown away his own goods. The man, the bystander, looked at me like I'd asked him why the sun comes up every morning. I'll always remember what he said.

"'Them tea-makers are standing up for what's theirs, kid. Better to go broke for freedom than to smile with someone's boot on your neck.'"

"Wow," Amelia said, listening with great interest. "Is that why you joined up, Calvin? To go broke in the fight?"

"I came here because John Penn's crew snuck into my house and gave me a really lopsided choice," Calvin admitted.

"That's how you got here. But that's not why you're here," Amelia said.

Calvin thought it over. "I guess to be honest I don't know why I'm here. Not just yet. But, well ..." he felt his face flush again as he met her eyes with his. "I found a reason to enjoy it, for what that's

85

worth."

There was a long silence between them. Amelia's cheeks really did go red and she looked away. "I know what you mean."

The pantry door swung open with a hard crack. Both of them jumped a mile as Commodore McCracken pushed his way inside, carrying two cured legs of pork. He almost dropped them both when he saw Calvin and Amelia in the enclosed space.

"Amelia! Why aren't you at the docks?" he snapped. Calvin didn't like how she flinched at her father's voice.

"I just, I was ...Calvin, he ...Brian made him come in here and he didn't know..."

"You were supposed to clean the shark mimic!" McCracken said.

"I did! It's already clean."

"Then clean something else. Go on, get!"

As Amelia scuttled out of the pantry, McCracken set his fiery gaze on Calvin. Calvin rooted himself to the spot, trying to convey some measure of courage, though his insides churned with uncertainty.

"And you," the old man seethed. "Stay away from my daughter, or you walk home. This is your only warning. Are we clear?"

"Crystal," Calvin said, fighting a tremble in his hands.

"Get out on the range. Now."

~

STAY AWAY FROM MY DAUGHTER.

ROCKEFELLER, GOODALL, AND WHITNEY

CHAPTER 6

Commodore McCracken changed Amelia's routine, and Calvin didn't see her for the rest of that week or the start of the next one. That wasn't to say that she was out of his head, though. He thought of her whenever his mind didn't need to be on the training at hand.

The days at Mount Vernon stretched on and on, melting into one continual push of brutal training that was occasionally interrupted by sleep. Brian and Peter kept running the recruits ragged, and a few of them reached their breaking point at the end of the first week. Calvin and the others woke up in time to beat the water buckets, and a quick headcount revealed that fewer than twenty recruits remained.

"Where do they go?" asked Stitch.

"They walk home," Edsel said.

"They say that, but that's not what they mean," Rusty said.

"That's what Pete told me." Edsel shrugged.

"Peter told you, but not us?" Cohen wondered aloud as he brushed chunks of mud out of his thick, sandy hair.

Edsel shrugged again. "Sure. I mean, we talk."

Calvin said nothing. Resentment welled up inside him—he was really starting to dislike Edsel, who had no shortage of talents. Whatever the McCracken brothers scribbled on their papers each day, the good of it was on Edsel's sheets. The way Calvin saw it, the rankings were only half about one's skills, and the other half was how well the trainers liked you personally. Calvin really wanted to beat Edsel, and he'd never do it by winning over the McCracken brothers. He'd have to do it with sheer grit, then.

While Calvin doubted he'd ever be as good at swimming as Edsel, he had risen to the top of the class in rifle shooting, he'd improved with the handguns to where he was just behind Edsel, and his agility among the rampaging swine was the talk of the dormitory. Word of this must have gotten back to the McCracken brothers—that, or Brian had gotten an earful from his father over allowing Calvin to be alone with Amelia—because they really stepped up their focus on Calvin.

"Another two hundred yards," Brian would say, once Calvin reached the end of the mile swim. "I saw you floating with the current back there."

Like hell you did, Calvin thought. But he choked back the words and swam the two hundred yards. He carried extra logs, lugged extra machinery, and ran extra miles every time they cracked the whip. Brian breathed down his neck the whole way, just waiting for Calvin to break. Fueled by pure spite, Calvin met each challenge. He wouldn't let this chump do him in.

He'd be lying to himself if he said part of his fuel wasn't Amelia. He sensed her eyes on him from time to time, watching from a mansion window, and whenever he thought of her, he pushed just a little harder.

*

Aside from physical conditioning, new opportunities arose for Calvin to prove his worth; after ten days at Mount Vernon, the McCracken brothers added classroom sessions to the recruits' schedules. Each cadet was issued a quill, ink bottle, and sheets of paper to take notes and study in the evenings. Stitch couldn't read or write, so he teamed up with Rusty, but Calvin helped him too. His mother had taught him to read at a young age, a skill which he hadn't always appreciated. Now it was another round in the cylinder.

Special instructors came in from other technomancer camps up and down the continent, teaching the recruits about various scientific disciplines that would give them an advantage over the mages. The first teacher was a bespectacled balding man named Bartholomew Rockefeller who specialized in chemistry. Calvin took notes about "accelerants" like gun powder, nitro glycerin, trinitrotoluene, and petroleum derivatives.

Once they got into petroleum, they learned about a wide load of uses for the bubbling black stuff, like how it was refined into different liquids for varied purposes. Rockefeller wanted the recruits to be able to identify the potent products based on smell and color alone. Before long most of the recruits had red eyes, runny noses, and ripping headaches from the fumes, and had to spend the rest of the session outside in the open air.

While going over his notes, Calvin reflected on how the mages used petroleum products to amplify the effects of some magical potions, while the technomancers used them to fuel and lubricate the engines on their mimics. The substance would be precious to both sides, if they went into a state of all-out war.

"Did you take good notes on the 'terramancy equations' he talked about?" Rusty asked, holding up her sheet of neatly-written notes. Calvin frowned.

"Terra-what?"

Rusty read from her paper. "He said the mages and mancers can use 'equations' with their magic to expand their senses. Terramancy helps them know where things are on the ground even if they can't see them. There's a way to counteract it, I think."

Calvin blushed a little. "I didn't catch that. I was trying to write down everything he said about petroleum."

"I bet you could counteract terramancy if you shoot the mage," Stitch said, shrugging his shoulders.

Rusty arched her eyebrows, then nodded and conceded the point. She and Calvin wrote that down.

*

The day after Rockefeller's class, they heard from a botanist named Shantewa Goodall. Ms. Goodall had them copy passages from her manuscript, *Herbs, Poxes & You,* and taught them how to identify useful foliage by the shapes of the leaves—some for medicines, others for poisons. The most common medicinal plant turned out to be tobacco, which went into poultices for disinfecting open wounds or healing bruises. Calvin had seen Brian use wads of the stuff on some of the cattle they kept on the grounds.

Miss Goodall also gave them a complicated recipe for a tincture called "crimbrose," an intense botanical cure-all which could counteract the effects of malpox. Calvin had heard of the disease before, by symptom rather than by name. It had spread through areas of Baltimore a few years back, killing hundreds. Miss Goodall told them that it still flared up in different places, and that if any of them showed symptoms of malpox, they were to immediately enter quarantine and begin a regiment of crimbrose infusions.

"Technomancers travel all across the continent. If you're contagious, you will only worsen the spread of this sickness," she explained.

That night Calvin asked Stitch if he knew what the word "quarantine" meant.

"Rusty said it's complete isolation. Kind of like being in the brig," Stitch said.

"Yeah, remember the brig, Calvin?" Edsel asked as he walked by, tailed by Lyla. She snickered at the jab. Calvin glared at him.

"I do, Edsel. They threw me down there for being too quick in the pigpen," he shot back. The look on Edsel's face confirmed a silent suspicion: it bugged him that Calvin was ahead of him in certain things.

Edsel just snorted and walked off with Lyla.

"I'm starting to not like him," Stitch said in a low voice. "Kind of a show-off."

"Don't worry about him," said Calvin, who worried about beating Edsel more than any of the other young recruits. "We were talking about isolation?

Stitch nodded. "Right. Quarantine. If you catch malpox, you might not get assigned to field duty, and that means no mimics."

"So what you're saying is, crimbrose is a good potion to know," Calvin said.

"Not a potion," Stitch warned, lowering his voice. "A concoction. Or an infusion. We don't make potions, man. That's for the Brits."

"Good point." Calvin filed the knowledge away and went to sleep.

*

After Miss Goodall's lecture, he expected a third day of lectures. Instead, the McCracken brothers took the cadets into the stables, where a large tarp covered something vaguely horse-shaped. Peter grabbed a handful of the cloth and yanked it aside to reveal a mechanical ...object. Calvin frowned as he tried to figure it out; maybe it had been a wolf at one point, but it lacked a lot of the armor panels that he'd seen on pictures of other, more complete mimics.

"This is an outdated model," Peter said. "The engineers tried making warg-mimics a few generations ago, but the walkers aren't as effective as the flying machines, so they phased them out. We use this one for practice. Your instructor today is a master mechanic named Horace Whitney. Give him your full attention."

Calvin took an instant liking to Horace, a rotund man with a wide mustache and perpetually grease-stained hands. He wore a full-body suit made of dark blue canvas, presumably to keep the rest of his body from getting dirty while he worked on the mimics, but it smelled of grime and oil, even in the stables. Horace didn't bother introducing himself further, or even going so far as to ask the recruits their names. He jumped right into his lecture and got to know the recruits along the way.

"These mimics are how we get monsters on our side. The mages can control biology, so we match them or beat them with technology." Horace slapped the dilapidated saddle on the back of the warg. "Engines, gear sets, transmissions, generators, pistons, actuators—all of these words are important mimic parts, and you should learn the basics before trying to operate one."

The basics turned out to be rather extensive. Calvin was

THESE MIMICS ARE HOW WE GET
MONSTERS ON OUR SIDE.

grouped with Stitch and Lyla, using tools like wrenches, screwdrivers, sockets, and other strangely named things to remove various parts and change out the damaged bits. Edsel's team focused on the gears and differential in the warg's hindquarters, and a silent race began between the two teams to see who could do it better.

Calvin's team got the engine back together first. While Edsel's team tried to put the gears in place, Calvin studied the ignition mechanism on the warg's control panel; it was a narrow slot filled with tiny pieces of metal that Horace called "tumblers," which fell into the different ridges of a key. Each mimic had a unique key, so that it couldn't be stolen or operated without the rider's permission. The whole concept fascinated Calvin, and he fiddled with it for half an hour.

The hands-on experience with the warg mimic helped them to prepare for classroom instruction on the larger mimics that the technomancers currently used in the field. Horace's lecture was short, as he was more inclined to practical instruction, and he soon bade farewell to the recruits, wishing them luck in their work. When the series of lectures ended, the McCracken brothers unveiled the greatest thing Calvin had ever seen in his life. They called it a "flight simulator." Having just come off a lecture about moving parts, his eyes naturally picked it apart to see what it did.

The McCrackens had retrofitted one whole room with a wide array of implements to reproduce different conditions of a mimic flight. One wall was covered with a taut white sheet, and the wall opposite featured a control booth with a "projector" inside. There was a pressurized chemical tank capped by hoses that snaked around the room, generating fake fog or smoke at the push of a button. Giant fans could create artificial wind, and a network of copper pipes rained down water from overhead.

All of this equipment surrounded a mimic sawhorse in the middle of the room, one without wings or an engine. All it had was a saddle and some handlebars with the standard controls of a dragonling mimic. It sat atop a thick spring that was bolted to the floor, and strong rubber cords pulled on it from four directions. Commodore McCracken himself sat up in the control booth and loaded a reel into the projector to show them how it worked. The recruits watched in intense silence as Peter manned the simulator controls and Brian mounted the sawhorse.

The room came alive. Images played on the screen wall, showing a mix of forest and sky racing past. Calvin blinked several times before he realized that this image must have been captured from a flying mimic at some previous time, then transmitted to the projector by whatever science the McCrackens used to make moving pictures. As the moving image veered left and down, Peter tugged on the controls that yanked the sawhorse to the left. Brian leaned into the turn, manipulating the handlebars as if he were atop a real mimic. Above the projector screen, a green lamp lit up.

"That means his response was correct," Peter explained.

Calvin looked up as the Commodore pulled some levers in the booth. Fog began to pour into the room. Rainwater followed, spraying down on Brian, who pulled himself tighter against the sawhorse. Peter worked the rubber cords hard, simulating very rough flying conditions. Whatever Brian did on the sawhorse, it set off a red light above the projection screen, followed by a blaring alarm. The sawhorse bucked violently and Brian was thrown onto a padded mat down below.

"And you can guess what that means," Peter said.

Calvin positively itched inside and out to get on that sawhorse. Out of the corner of his eye he saw Edsel wringing his fingers and shifting from foot to foot. Jealousy bubbled inside him, and Calvin recommitted to beating Edsel. There was no way that anything Edsel had done in his life prior to being recruited would give him an edge on the flight simulator.

Still, when Brian and Peter assigned numbers to the recruits at random—their turn on the simulator—Calvin didn't resent coming up after Edsel in line. He figured it would be good for him to see a few others try it, see what their mistakes were, and then evaluate Edsel from there, so that he could really trounce him when his own time came.

The most common problem that the recruits had was keeping their weight centered over the sawhorse when they leaned into the turns. They had no way of strapping themselves in, and unlike a horse, the saddle on the mimic didn't have stirrups, just metal pegs with the pedals that controlled the wing flaps. Calvin studied the main body of the sawhorse, especially the shape of the fuel tank on top, and figured that if he squeezed his thighs tightly together when he leaned, he could hold himself up without having to rest his weight on the handlebars—an action that frequently resulted in the recruits over-steering or over-revving the lifter fans, sending them into a sideways spiral. Peter warned them several times that such an action atop a real mimic would most likely result in a "wipeout" at high speeds, from high up.

"What's a wipeout?" Avery whispered.

"You either die, or wish you had," Edsel grunted. "Seen a man come off a horse at full gallop, and he was in severe pain for days. Imagine falling out of the sky! Of course, the secret is to..."

Calvin tuned out the rest, unwilling to listen to another bloated Edsel lecture.

Cohen and Stitch did okay on their first turns, which lasted about ten minutes apiece. Rusty held on out of sheer stubbornness even when the red lights flashed and the simulation ended. When Brian tried to pry her off the sawhorse, she stiff-armed him and jerked her hips sideways, righting the thing.

"I ride horses, okay? I can do this."

Thoroughly peeved, Brian cast a glance at the Commodore up in the control booth. McCracken only smiled, amused at Rusty's grit, and Calvin silently cheered her on.

Edsel handled his first run rather skillfully, though it seemed to Calvin that the McCracken brothers didn't pull the rubber cords very hard—especially not as hard as they did when Calvin's turn came. Before he'd really settled his feet onto the pegs the sawhorse collapsed onto its right side, the right front cord having gone totally slack. Calvin's knees bit painfully into the sawhorse's flanks, just like he'd envisioned, and he pulled himself tight against the fuel tank to hold on.

"Whoops," Brian said. He didn't sound sorry.

Ride it out, Calvin thought. Brian was only going to make him better.

Exactly what he needed.

He righted the sawhorse and went at it anew.

*

After their session in the simulator, Commodore McCracken revealed a leader board with the cadets' names across the top, and an aggregate score based on their performance in various areas: handguns, long rifles, the blunderbuss, the physical training, and the flight simulator. For their group, Calvin and Edsel were at the top, though it was rather close. They were at seventy-six and seventy-eight, respectively. It was their numbers in the simulator that brought them down. Calvin would have to get better at that.

The McCrackens then sent the cadets to a class on "orienteering." Each recruit was issued a compass and a map of the continent, and then learned how to navigate from place to place using just their instruments. Calvin thought it tedious; he only took an interest in it when Stitch pointed out that they would need these skills to fly mimics, because technomancers mostly moved in the dark, like John Penn and his crew.

Calvin's head swam with all the new information he had absorbed. At night he dreamt of the flight simulator, and he found himself itching to get back at it the next day.

It wasn't on the morning itinerary; instead they went back to the stables where Peter had laid out sixteen identical black knives on a table, bidding each of them to take one. Calvin looked around and did a head count—sure enough, they were down to just sixteen cadets. More had washed out in previous days. He wondered where they were now.

"These knives are made of a special blend of metal," Peter explained. "We call it 'frosted iron.' The mages' spells break down in the presence of this metal. You can use them for just about anything."

Calvin recalled the farm raid, stabbing the enchanted lock with Brian's knife.

Avery held his knife up to the light. "Surface could be a little smoother. Edge isn't great either. Wouldn't be great at hunting or skinning."

"Unless you're hunting mages, right?" Edsel smiled at his own joke.

Cohen studied his knife more closely. "This is coated with silver, isn't it? That's where the texture comes from. It's silver dust."

"Correct. That's one of the rarest metals on the continent. After the iron is coated, it's treated in a gas chamber with another element called krypton. Very complex process, and we're lucky to have discovered it," said Peter.

"Stab a mage with this and his power will drop. Strike a blood vessel and he'll lose his magic for days, even weeks. Stab him in the heart and he's not coming back," Brian said.

They practiced different knife-fighting techniques on wooden dummies and posts, which had been hacked at and stabbed and shaved by countless previous recruits. As Calvin went through the motions on the dummy, he thought of what Amelia had said in the pantry—lots of recruits leave, none ever come back. The people who'd left these marks in years past ...where were they now? How many of them ever got to cut the enemy?

Was this training really working?

He wouldn't know unless he got the chance to use it in the field. Holding this in his mind, he went to work on the dummy, committing the movements to memory.

Brian ended the day's training and sent them to the dining hall in the mansion for dinner. As Calvin trudged to the house, Stitch chatted him up about the knives and how they would fare in a real fight. Calvin only half heard him; he was looking up at the windows, looking at Amelia, who'd pulled a curtain partway open and risked a wave at him. She had her hair braided into two tails, just like the day she'd brought him extra rations in the brig, and her golden-yellow blouse gave her a kind of glow against the colorful sunset. He just smiled, fighting the urge to wave back and raise suspicion. She disappeared, but her lingering image in his mind left him with a pleasant warmth.

Seventeen days had passed since his arrival at Mount Vernon. The feeling had snuck up on him, but as Calvin reflected on the past two and a half weeks, he felt like a different person—his *own* person; a more capable version of the boy who had left Baltimore. Maybe this was what it felt like to be a technomancer. As he drifted to sleep that night, he wondered how he had ever lived so long as a plain old duffer.

*

Saturday came. Peter announced that they would spend more time in the simulator starting on Monday, with the cadets being broken up into groups of four, and then assigned to the room in different shifts. Calvin could think of nothing else all day, even as they ran through Brian's intense new forest obstacle course. It involved lots of sprinting, crawling, climbing, rolling through mud, keeping one's weapons in order, and firing straight when tired. As had become the norm, Calvin and Edsel gravitated toward each other and silently pushed themselves harder, eager to exploit the other's shortcomings.

The distance-running portion of the course brought them back to the training camp, scratched, filthy, tired, and hungry. Brian prodded the stragglers along, while Calvin and Edsel found reserves of energy to run all-out to the finish. They were so engrossed in the competition that they didn't hear Brian screaming for everyone to take cover.

"Gryphon rider!" he bellowed. Calvin didn't notice until Peter threw a rock to get their attention, and he glanced back to see an object in the sky, getting larger by the second.

"The house!" Brian said, urging everyone to the mansion.

The stables were on the far side of the estate, and a mad dash for the horse stalls would leave them exposed.

"No time—the tarps! Go for the tarps!" Peter bellowed.

The cadets scattered. Last week Brian and Peter had shown them hidden tarps all over the grounds, painted and disguised so that from above they would look like the terrain. Rusty and Stitch took cover together under one tarp—usually only large enough to protect two—and everyone else buddied up in like fashion. Edsel, who had already run off into the trees, left Calvin on his own.

The gryphon flew so close that Calvin could make out the details of the rider's harness. Desperate for cover, Calvin spotted an outcropping of rock to his left, surrounded by berry bushes. He remembered that there was a tarp there, and when he dove under it, he collided with someone who had already taken shelter there.

Amelia.

"Hi!" she whispered, throwing the tarp over him.

"What are you doing out here?"

"Stuff. Hush!"

They both went deathly still at the sound of flapping wings high above the tree line.

"What's going on?" Calvin whispered.

"Scouts. They come through here sometimes. They can't see the grounds for what they are, but you guys aren't covered by the same guises. Hard to explain," Amelia said.

"Shouldn't you be in the mansion, though?"

"What, aren't you glad to see me?" Amelia asked in falsetto,

WHAT ARE YOU DOING OUT HERE?

sticking out her lip.

"Of course I am." He was glad for the mud on his face, so she couldn't see him blush. Not that there was much light under the tarp.

"If my brothers ask, I was picking berries."

"And the real story?"

"Playing with Father's personal mimic," Amelia grinned.

"There's one out here? I've been all over these woods and I haven't seen one."

"It's hidden. I really shouldn't talk about it, so keep it a secret, okay?"

"I will. Promise." He sniffed. "Something smells good. Not these berries, either."

"Probably this." Amelia rummaged around and produced a

leather pouch full of herbs and leaves and flower petals. "I actually *was* gathering things—I put different fragrances into the soaps in our lavatory. My mother taught me how."

"I've heard of lavatories, but I've never seen a proper one. Where I'm from, we just bathe with buckets," Calvin said.

"I could show you sometime. When we're alone, I mean."

"We are alone," Calvin pointed out.

"Not like this. Although..." she trailed off when her big round eyes met his, and he was suddenly aware of how close she was, how nice she smelled, how her blue eyes lit up even in the shade of the tarp—and how alone they were.

Amelia closed her eyes. Calvin copied her. He gravitated toward her lips.

A hand tore the tarp back. "Adler! The rider's gone ...hey!"

Calvin and Amelia leapt away from each other, but the damage was done. Brian McCracken loomed over them, furious. He grabbed Calvin's collar in both hands and hefted him to his feet with one pull.

"Brian, no!" Amelia shrieked.

"My old man told you to bug off of my sister!" Brian roared.

"Or what?" Calvin snarled back, taking Brian by the wrists.

Brian rammed his forehead into Calvin's nose. The shocking crack and ensuing numbness disoriented Calvin for a second, allowing Brian to recover and tackle him around the waist, pushing him deeper into the bushes.

Calvin was having none of it. He planted his feet and wrapped his own arms around Brian's torso, then sank into a crouch and leaned back. Heaving mightily, Calvin grunted and pulled Brian off his feet. In a panic Brian released Calvin all too late—Calvin spiked him into the ground, the same way he used to wrestle with ornery rams at home.

CALVIN ENDURED IT WELL...

Brian recovered fast. He was on his feet instantly, and the fight went to blows. In this Brian was quicker and more experienced, but Calvin endured it well and got in close where Brian's haymaker punches couldn't get any momentum.

After a brief moment of grappling and punching they fell to

the ground and rolled through the thicket, earning several cuts and scratches from the sharp branches. When they stopped, Calvin was atop Brian who was face down in the mud with one arm wrenched behind his back.

Silence smothered all of Mount Vernon, all save for Calvin and Brian's ragged breathing. That was when Calvin felt dozens of eyes on him. The other cadets stood in a wide circle around the bushes, staring in open-mouthed amazement.

Peter shoved his way between Stitch and Edsel, fixing Calvin with almost the same alarmed expression as Amelia. Immediately Calvin released Brian and got up, allowing the younger McCracken brother to come up for air.

Calvin just *knew* there'd be hell to pay for beating one of the trainers in front of the other cadets.

~

TECHNOMANCER JACK BADGETT

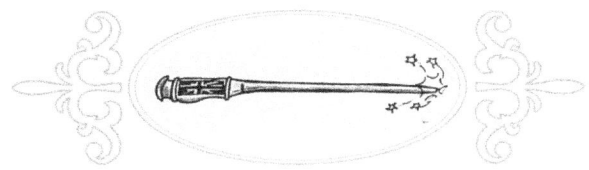

CHAPTER 7

"How are you not in the brig right now?" Stitch stared at Calvin in awe. Everyone had returned to the dormitories after washing up. Calvin sat on the corner of his bed and went about cleaning his equipment, lips pursed, eyes unblinking. Rusty and Avery flanked Stitch expectantly, as if Calvin had an answer for his question. He didn't.

"No idea, man."

Peter had ordered Calvin and the other cadets to get cleaned up. Brian had left without a word. Calvin was sure the elder McCracken brother had seen the whole mess play out. Both brothers in the end were more upset that their sister had been caught out on the grounds. Calvin wondered if they knew about her playing in the Commodore's mimic—wherever it was.

"Well, you *should* be in the brig. That was way over the line, Adler," Edsel said, taking a horsehair brush to his boots.

"Ain't your call, Ed," Rusty chided, craning her neck to look him in the eye.

"And? Just because you don't like the person telling you a truth doesn't mean they're wrong," Edsel said, pointing the brush at her.

"The brig's not so bad." Calvin fixed Edsel with a hard look.

"Maybe the second time will straighten you out," Edsel said. Calvin noticed Cohen and Lyla hanging around by him, like kids to a ram. He narrowed his eyes—so, it was to be like this?

Not important right now.

A fleeting movement in the doorway caught Calvin's attention, and he stared through it to the mansion beyond. When would the McCrackens come back to punish him? And what of Amelia? That question nagged him even worse than any ache or pain in his body, worse even than Edsel's twittering. Was Jonathan McCracken chewing her out for talking to Calvin? He couldn't bear the thought of her being punished for that. What did the old man have against Calvin anyway? Good enough to fight a war, but not good enough to make his daughter happy?

Any one of a thousand well-imagined punishments swam through Calvin's head as he meticulously cleaned his gear, changed into fresh fatigues and stretched his toes before putting his boots on and getting into bed. Stitch, Rusty, and Avery kept hanging around and chattering about the fight, which did nothing to help clear Calvin's head, but he stayed silent. Any moment now he expected one of the McCracken brothers to drag him outside with orders to "walk home."

The order never came.

*

Sleep had finally taken him after midnight, but only held him for a quarter of an hour before a frightening noise filled the training grounds and pried every cadet from bed. Calvin snapped awake and his hand flew to his waist, snatching up the frosted iron knife. In the mental fog, he picked out a sound that his heart had learned well: the buzz of a mimic's engine.

"You hear that? Sounds like a machine," Stitch said a second later.

Rusty groaned and rubbed sleep from her eyes. Stitch put a brotherly arm around her shoulder and led her to the door as Calvin ran outside, gaining speed. In the moonlight he spotted Edsel right on his heels.

Prat, Calvin thought.

Following the noise, Calvin picked out a weak light moving across the blackened sky, getting closer. He and Edsel pointed at it together. While Edsel declared to the others that he'd seen it first, Calvin's eyes grew wide.

The mimic was coming straight for them.

It dropped down low and closed in fast. He would half-regret it later, but Calvin turned and knocked Edsel to the ground just as the machine whooshed overhead, hammering them with a blast of underwing pressure. The other cadets also leapt comically out of the mimic's path as it plowed into the open stables, where it puttered to a halt.

"Whoa! What!" Stitch shouted.

Calvin was up and running to the barn in an instant. Dust settled in the darkness; Edsel told Avery and Lyla to light the lanterns. To Calvin's dismay, they obeyed. Not only was he talking down to Calvin, he was gaining a following? Calvin wasn't sure what to do about that.

Soft yellow light pushed away the darkness, revealing two new gutters that had been dug into the stable's soft dirt floor, courtesy of the mimic's landing gear. For its part, the mimic had landed on its feet, tipped forward with the nose almost touching the ground. Calvin took in the magnificent little machine, noting the familiar sawhorse body, fuel tank, handlebar controls, a short glass windshield, and a scaled metal neck ending in a sculpted cowl meant to look like a dragon's head. Two short gun barrels jutted out beneath the neck, just over the air intake. A pair of wings with built-in lifter fans spread out from the flanks, and a short tail stabbed out of the back end.

He was smitten with it instantly. For having just come in on a rough landing, it looked to be in great shape, ready to fly again. Its rider hadn't fared so well; he had flown over the handlebars and lay in a heap several feet beyond his machine, illuminated by the flickering headlight.

Bradley

Calvin and Edsel rushed over to him. A foul odor assaulted Calvin's nostrils and he gagged before he could reach the man. Covering his nose, he coughed and took a step back. Not even Edsel's showmanship could propel him the rest of the way.

"Sweet simmering cesspool, what the hell is that smell?" Edsel wheezed through his fingers.

"He's been cursed." Calvin took a closer look, braving the stench by hooking the collar of his tunic over his nose. The rider lay groaning on his back, mostly covered by his flying leathers. At his throat and face—where his skin was exposed—huge, swollen purple boils glistened in the lantern light. His hair was a shock of white fibers, glowing bright all on their own.

"Someone was chasing him?" Edsel guessed.

HE'S BEEN CURSED...

115

"Bet it was that faunamancer we saw earlier. The one on the gryphon," Calvin said.

"It makes sense. A gryphon could follow that stench through a hurricane. And his hair would light up the night from quite a distance! They must have gotten close and cursed him before he opened the throttle and bailed," Edsel said.

Calvin took a knee beside the rider, who raised a beckoning hand toward him. "Hey. What's your name?" Calvin asked.

The rider only managed a gurgling noise.

Behind Calvin, Rusty cried out in alarm at something on the mimic.

"Have mercy! You guys, this is Jack Badgett!" she said.

Badgett? Why do I know that name? Calvin thought.

Avery approached Calvin, Edsel, and the man Jack Badgett. "Definitely cursed," Avery said. "I've seen this before, the night John Penn recruited me. Badgett's not going to survive."

Badgett coughed and suppressed a whimper.

"Cohen, Lyla, go tell the McCrackens," Edsel said. "Maybe we can help Badgett."

"What can I get you? What do you need?" Calvin whispered, taking Badgett's outstretched hand. The man's body slackened, like he was relieved.

"Take ...care..." he gasped. "Good machine." With his free hand, he pointed at the mimic.

"I will," Calvin promised.

Peter and Brian burst into the stables a second later; it seemed they'd already been on their way. They took one look at the mimic, another at Badgett, then scooped him up in a two-man carry—taking care with a pouch that was strapped to his jacket—and hurried back to the house without a word. Calvin's blood pumped harder as Brian brushed past him, but still the McCrackens said nothing about the fight that afternoon. This business with Jack Badgett must be dead serious.

"Man, I can't believe it. That was Jack Badgett," Stitch muttered again, looking out the door after Peter and Brian.

"How did you know it was him?" Calvin asked. Stitch pointed to the leather saddle on the dragonling mimic. Calvin came closer and read an inscription that had been burned into the side with a branding iron.

JACK BADGETT: ACE MERYKAN.

"What does 'Ace Merykan' mean?" asked Avery.

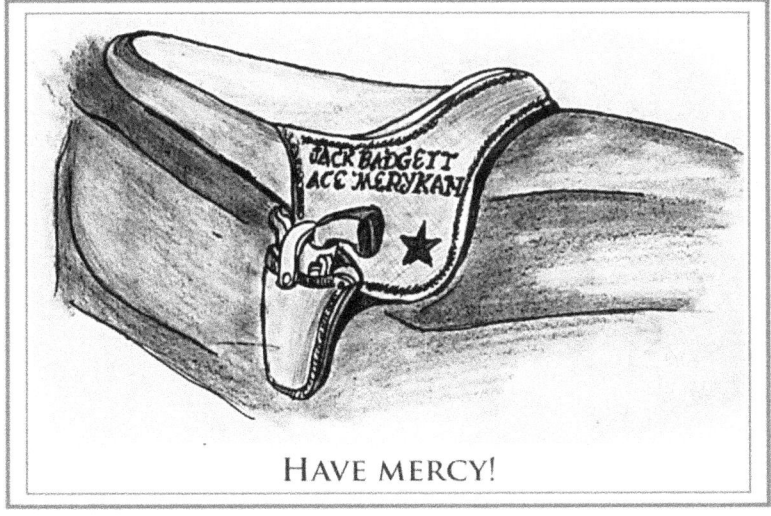

HAVE MERCY!

"You've never heard the Brits say 'Meryka'?" Rusty said, surprised. "That's what they call the continent. The explorer who found and mapped the place was called Richard Ap Meryk, so they named it after him."

"You mean they didn't name it after the king and queen?" thought Calvin aloud.

"They named other places for them. Georgia, Virginia, Maryland ..."

"Got it." Calvin trailed off as he ran his fingers down the soft saddle. Parts of it were worn smooth from overuse. The paint had rubbed off on the sides of the fuel tank, right where Jack's padded knees would have squeezed it countless times while turning. The controls were also well-worn, and one of the gauges had a cracked glass face on it.

Amazing. Badgett had told *him* to take care of it. Calvin wanted nothing else in the world than to be charged with this mimic's care.

"The Brits only call us 'Merykans' when they mean it as an insult," Stitch said.

"So?" Edsel said, sounding anxious to get in on the topic. "I think Badgett has the right idea. He wears it with pride. I will probably do it too when they give me a mimic."

"You'll be waiting a while. They'll send me out on this one," Calvin said.

"Ha! Not likely."

"That or I'll just take it."

Edsel fixed him with a hard look. Stitch intervened.

"Tough doing, that. Peter took the key."

Calvin broke eye contact with Edsel long enough to confirm this. The ignition slot was empty. Emboldened by an idea, he went to the workbench at the end of the stable and retrieved a few fine-tipped tools.

"What are you doing?" Edsel demanded. Calvin ignored him, fiddling with the ignition until the tumblers were in place, then he twisted it to the side and held it. Nothing happened.

"It's because you..." Edsel began.

"Just shut up, okay? It's not in neutral. I got it." Calvin squeezed in the clutch and clicked the shifter pedal until it hit the soft spot between first and second gears. Then he turned the ignition switch again. It clicked several times, set off a small *boom* that rattled the saddle, and then coughed to life. Stitch and Rusty cheered him on, along with other recruits who had followed the commotion into the stables. Edsel clearly didn't like that.

"Okay, we're all very impressed, but you don't know how to handle this thing. Move over." Edsel put a hand on Calvin's shoulder and leaned into him, trying to get him out of the saddle.

"Get your hand off me," Calvin warned.

"Get off the mimic!" Edsel growled, putting his full weight into the attempt. Gripping the saddle with his knees, Calvin rammed the heel of his hand hard into Edsel's chin and sent him sprawling into the dirt.

"You're not an officer!" Calvin barked.

Abandoning all pretense of decency, Edsel recovered and

charged at Calvin, roaring with rage. The two recruits fell over the idling mimic and hit the ground in a heap, punching and grappling with each other to the amazement and entertainment of their peers.

The fight went on for a few seconds until Peter returned with a two-gallon can of liquid odor neutralizer—for the chaser curse that

YOU'RE NOT AN OFFICER!

Badgett had brought with him—and the elder McCracken brother pulled them off of each other.

"Why is this mimic idling?" Peter demanded.

"He did it!" Edsel cried, thrusting a finger at Calvin. "I tried to stop him."

"Right, you lying twit," Rusty said.

Peter produced the key from his pocket, shoved it into the ignition and turned it off. "You and you, the brig. Now," he said to Calvin and Edsel. He thrust the can at Stitch. "Douse the area where Badgett was, and then the rest of you get back to the dorm-

-itory. Dismissed."

Fuming, Calvin glared at Edsel as Peter herded them to the mansion. There seemed to be no shortage of people to hate at Mount Vernon.

*

They spent the night in different cells. Amelia did not come to visit. The next day, Brian retrieved them both and ordered them to the shores of the Potomac River.

Calvin stood on the muddy bank in his bare feet, wearing only a thin pair of shorts, a tight undershirt, and a watertight oilskin pack. Inside it were his rifle (in three pieces), his frosted iron knife, and two cylinders of ammunition. Twelve rounds in all. Beside him, Edsel wore the exact same outfit and carried an identical bag with identical contents.

"Do not misunderstand the severity of this punishment," Commodore McCracken growled. "There will be no more quarrels between cadets, and there will be absolutely no operating of mimics without proper authorization, and I'll be strung up by my own entrails before I tolerate any of you lying to the officers!"

Calvin sensed Edsel tightening up. That single act was the only reason why Calvin wasn't about to endure this punishment alone.

The Commodore turned to the line of recruits behind him, all in fatigues and boots. "Let this be a lesson to you as well, that you will share this fate if you break any of these rules during the time that remains you. Peter? Sound off."

Peter stepped up as Commodore McCracken retreated to the

mansion, never looking back. Calvin still ached to know what Brian had said to him about yesterday. Why hadn't Calvin been punished for that yet? It was a pressing concern that would have to wait.

"The requirements are simple," Peter said. "On the opposite bank of the Potomac, near Piscataway Creek, there lies an old submersible. It floats—kind of. You will swim there, retrieve the damaged submersible and return it to the naval yard at Dogue Creek on this side of the river."

"Why don't we just swim back, too?" Edsel puffed out his chest a little, knowing that he was the better swimmer. Calvin rolled his eyes.

"Because you won't be returning empty-handed. And don't give me any more cheek. You will regret it," Peter warned.

Edsel swallowed hard. Calvin suppressed a smirk.

Peter continued. "You will need the submersible to bring back your haul. Before you are allowed to return, you must catch and kill thirty pounds of meat. That's thirty pounds apiece. If you come back without the meat or without the submersible, you will walk home. Are we clear?"

The words weighed on him, and Calvin understood the severity of the punishment. "Walking home" was definitely something bad. How bad, though?

Had the dismissed recruits been executed?

"What are you waiting for?" Peter chided. "Daylight's burning."

Stitch and Rusty flashed a thumbs-up to Calvin, who nodded

discreetly in return. Then he jumped in the river.

~

PETER MCCRACKEN

CHAPTER 8

Calvin had no misgivings about his ability to swim across the river, even in such minimal clothing. While that made it easier to paddle with the bag on his back, he knew it would cause problems once he had to stomp through the woods. Though Edsel was equally handicapped, he beat Calvin to the shore by minutes, assembled his rifle and disappeared into the trees while Calvin was pulling himself up the bank.

Fingers buzzing with exhaustion—he had only slept a few hours in the brig—he took a minute to catch his breath before he headed into the brush without putting his weapon together. He would wait for his hands to dry first.

As Peter had warned, daylight burned. High noon was upon

125

him when he saw his first target: a fat wild turkey pecking about in the brush. Taking great care to keep quiet, Calvin shrugged out of his pack and pieced the rifle together, muffling the *click* of its various components by tucking it against his stomach and folding himself over the weapon. Cylinder in place, he pulled back the hammer, lined up the sights, and shot the turkey straight through the neck at two hundred yards.

The *crack* of his bullet would scare off other game in the area for a while, so he retrieved the heavy bird—at least a twenty-pounder—and lugged it through the woods by its feet while searching for his next target. An hour later he found two more wild turkeys; one he shot directly in the face, scaring the other one into a frantic retreat. Calvin took two deep breaths, let them out slow, pulled the hammer again and followed the turkey in a westerly direction. Adjusting for movement, he squeezed the trigger.

A puff of red, and the turkey tripped over itself as it died. Once Calvin retrieved all three of the hefty fowls, he admired his handiwork: headshots, the three of them. None of the really hearty meat would be damaged.

"Top that, Edsel," Calvin muttered. He gathered up the three birds—a good sixty pounds altogether!—and started back to the shore, intending to follow it north to the broken submersible. Once out in the open, the sound of gunfire close by made him fall to the ground and cover his head. Then he remembered that Edsel was still out there somewhere, wasting bullets.

Fuming, Calvin kept count of the echoing shots: six in all.

Edsel had wasted a whole cylinder? Surely he wasn't that bad of a shot.

Then came the scream.

At first he thought it was Edsel, but the sound was too high, even for him, even in a full panic. The hellish howling sound didn't bear the mark of fear, but rather of fury, and somewhere in the back of his mind he remembered his father warning of massive woodland cats called *painters* that lived in the trees south of Maryland.

Calvin was running through the woods before he could give it a second thought. He left the turkeys behind, swapping cylinders in his rifle so that he had six live rounds instead of three. The howling came from straight ahead, and as he neared the sound he thought he could make out Edsel shrieking. Calvin burst through a stand of shrubbery and into a small clearing, staring up at Edsel who was cowering in a tree fifteen feet off the ground, rifle strapped to his back.

And beneath him prowled the biggest damn cat Calvin had ever laid eyes on.

Fully ten feet long from nose to tail, its body one long coil of liquid muscle under taut skin, the ferocious beast limped back and forth on three good legs, howling up at Edsel in a rage. One of its rear legs glistened, covered in blood. So Edsel had gotten a shot off at the thing, but why had he stowed his rifle? To climb? Sure, but why didn't he use it now?

Something silver glinted in the sun, almost directly beneath the painter, and then Calvin understood: it was a spare cylinder. Edsel was out of ammo.

If Calvin thought that the painter's injury had somehow hindered it, he was sorely wrong. The cat saw him and switched targets, bounding through the underbrush like a streak of black lighting. Calvin popped off two frantic rounds and then the cat was on him, shoving him onto his back, trying to sink its three-inch fangs into his neck. Calvin gasped and spun the rifle sideways, jamming the barrel into the cat's wide open jaws, exerting every last ounce of strength to leverage the cat's head away from his face.

Knifelike claws sliced into Calvin's forearms, hooking into his soft flesh. Calvin screamed again, feeling a fresh new flame of fear and agony deep in his bowels. Was this it? Was this how he would die, shredded by a beast that outweighed him with muscle and outclassed him with sheer ferocity?

Fear triggered an onslaught of random memories that flashed through his head like a moving picture, which was interrupted when Edsel dropped to the ground and retrieved his spare cylinder. The cat thrashed and tore at Calvin, trying to get its open maw around his throat. Face contorted with savage anger, Edsel loaded the cylinder, jammed the tip of the rifle into the cat's ear and squeezed the trigger over and over, until the cylinder clicked empty. The heavy cat went slack and collapsed atop Calvin, no longer tugging at his bleeding arms.

"Thank you," Edsel said, panting heavily.

"Help," Calvin wheezed under the cat's weight. He could

EDSEL DROPPED TO THE GROUND...

barely hear his own voice through the ringing in his ears.

"Oh, yeah." Edsel dropped his rifle and crouched down, leaning into the cat's flank. Together they shoved it aside, and Calvin carefully worked the monster's claws out of his flesh.

"Thank you," Edsel said again. "Damn thing came out of nowhere." He kicked his rifle. "Now I'm out of rounds, all I got was one turkey. And this cat, I guess."

Calvin breathed hard, trying not to give into an impending sense of shock. "Too heavy. No way can we carry it."

"I know ...can I borrow some rounds? Do you have any left? Not that there'll be any more birds in these parts."

"Forget it. You can have one of my birds."

Edsel's mouth popped open. "You serious?"

"I'm pretty much done out here, aren't you?" Calvin tore his shirt into bandages and tried to wrap his forearms.

"It's better if you let the muscles go slack, or you'll agitate the laceration," Edsel said, using the condescending tone that had so far grated on Calvin's every nerve. He didn't have it in him to get angry, though; Edsel at least knew what he was talking about, and was willing to help him tie up his wounds.

"Thanks," Calvin said with a sigh.

"You too. You don't like me, Adler. I get that."

"You're keen that way."

Edsel actually laughed as he worked. "Fair assessment. Guess I could be easier to get along with if I tried. Sometimes I wonder if that's how people were in George Washington's time. Maybe they'd have beaten the mages back then if they weren't too busy annoying each other."

"Woulda saved us a headache, at least." Calvin opened and closed the fingers on one hand after Edsel tied off the bandages.

"That gonna work for you?" Edsel asked.

"It'll do. Let's do the other, and get out of here."

Once finished, Edsel retrieved a smaller turkey from the brush, took up both their rifles, and followed Calvin back the direction that he'd come, and they set off in search of the submersible.

*

THE OLD SUBMERSIBLE

"And then to top it all off, the stupid thing was pedal-powered," Calvin said.

"No engine?" Stitch asked, preparing a tobacco poultice for Calvin's mangled forearms. Though his skin had been cut to shreds, the cat hadn't sliced through any major muscles or tendons. Calvin would be sore, injured for a few days, but not maimed.

"Nope. And it was taking on water. Half the time, Edsel was cranking the pumps to keep us from sinking. My arms were useless so I just sat there and manned the pedals," Calvin said.

"Must have been an old mimic," Rusty said. "The first generation was pedal-powered, remember?" They had studied it in class.

"This thing wasn't even a mimic. It was just a basic machine, and a lousy one at that. No shape to it at all." Calvin sighed.

"Well, I hope you learned your lesson, whatever that was," Stitch muttered.

Calvin looked over at Edsel's bunk. Edsel was up at the mansion, talking to the McCrackens. "Guess we'll see," he said.

*

He awoke in the middle of the night with a soft hand over his mouth. A gentle whisper in his ear disarmed him; he could never draw a weapon on the voice's owner.

"Amelia," he breathed.

"Hi," she murmured. "I heard you got hurt today. Come on." She tugged the sheets off of him, exposing his boots and fatigues. She bade him follow her up to the house, and he did, exhausted though he was.

Wearing a long nightgown and boots of her own, Amelia took him by the hand and led him through a side entrance, down a corridor he hadn't yet explored, up a winding staircase to the second floor. The door to the left was cracked open, and flickering candlelight made the shadows dance on the rug before them.

Calvin followed her in, and as he looked around, he realized that she was fulfilling her promise to show him a lavatory.

The lush room had many marble and porcelain fixtures, including a wash basin, a tub large enough to fit a person inside it, and something that Amelia identified as a "water closet." Bottles of various substances dotted the counter, some for grooming, others for medical attention.

"How are you doing?" she asked, looking up into his eyes.

"Better now," he admitted. She beamed.

"Sit. And take your boots off, be comfortable. Let me see your arms."

"How did you know it was my arms?"

"I overheard Edsel telling my brothers what had happened on the other side of the river. He said a painter got its claws in you!" Amelia helped him out of his tunic, exposing his bandaged arms. The yellowed strips of cloth smelled of tobacco. She gasped at the sight of his mangled skin.

"What else did Edsel say?" Calvin asked.

Amelia recounted the debriefing. To Edsel's credit, he had told the story with complete accuracy, save for one thing: his second turkey was supposedly Calvin's third, and according to Edsel, they had shot the bird at the same time, which explained the number of holes in it. In truth, Edsel's first bird had been shot through three times, as he was a lousy hunter and didn't know to aim for the head.

"Ah!" Calvin winced as Amelia dabbed at his wounds with a

clear, sharp-smelling liquid. "Is that alcohol?"

"Yes. I know it burns, but it will disinfect the wound better than the tobacco will. Won't make so much pus this way," she said.

"I think I might prefer the pus," Calvin said through clenched teeth as Amelia sterilized a deep gash over a yellowing bruise.

"Sorry," she said. He felt the soft tips of her fingers brush his shoulder, gently stroking an uninjured section of his skin. Calvin's ears flushed hot.

"Oh, it's fine." He breathed out, suddenly less aware of his wounds, even as she continued to treat them.

"So, I'm curious," Amelia said after a moment's silence. "I had to clean and dress those four turkeys this evening. Some for cooking, others for salting. Three had their heads shot right off, and the other took three rounds through the breast—the best meat. Three rounds from the same angle, I might add."

"Yes?"

"I don't think you and Edsel shot the same bird at the same time. Not unless you were shoulder-to-shoulder when you did it. I've seen you at target practice, Cal. He's better with the revolver and you're better with the rifle. It's not hard to figure out who killed which birds."

The silence returned. Calvin didn't know how he should respond, and he was desperately afraid of sounding full of himself. Mount Vernon got enough of that just by having Edsel around, truce or not.

"Why did you do it? Give him your bird, I mean," she asked.

"I don't know," Calvin admitted, shaking Edsel out of his thoughts. "The easy answer? I just wanted to get out of there. I was injured, I was tired, I was done. But ...I feel like even if I had killed the cat before it hurt me, I might still have shared with Edsel. He's annoying, but at the end of the day we're on the same side. It felt like the right thing to do."

Amelia smiled bashfully, studying her work on his arms. She smeared a thick, clear gel over the claw marks and wrapped them in clean new bandages. "I think that's what I like about you, Calvin Adler. You do things because they're right. That's good."

Calvin took her hand in his. "I think I have a lot of reasons why I like you," he said.

Amelia leaned in close. "Here's one more," she whispered, brushing her lips against his, letting them touch all too briefly before she broke away. Fire shot through him, filling him with vigor. He felt alive, whole, ready for action, and he knew it had nothing to do with the medicine. He'd even closed his eyes without realizing it, and an almost inaudible breath jumped out of his chest.

"Only one more?" he whispered, fingers trembling.

The corners of her mouth reached into a wide smile and her eyes lit up bright. She bit her lip and leaned in again, too slow for his liking. Calvin rested a hand on the basin and leaned in, pushing his lips hungrily against hers and holding them there for as long as the fire in his chest would allow.

Time melted away. There was no training, no army, no mage war to be fought, nothing beyond the lavatory door that mattered to him. His fingers seemed to pull his hand to her waist, sliding carefully around to the small of her back, waiting after every inch as if to be sure he had permission. She only kissed him with greater fervor, slipping her palms over his shoulders and brushing the tips of her fingers over the bumps in his muscles. When he'd kissed her long enough to start worrying whether he was taking too much, he pulled back and smiled wide enough for it to hurt. As for Amelia, she exuded a light all her own as she let her fingers trail down his arms so she could take his hands in hers.

"I liked that," she giggled.

"Yeah, I can't say that was a problem." Had he really just said that?

They stayed there for a minute more, until a bump in the hallway made them both jump, and they realized what kind of trouble they'd be in if they were discovered. Calvin exercised superhuman willpower and extricated his hands from hers, then fumbled with his tunic. Amelia blushed and looked to the side, busying herself with replacing the bottles she'd used on his wounds.

Once finished, she led Calvin out of the lavatory and back outside. Neither of them noticed the door across the hallway, opened to a narrow slit, where Peter McCracken sat with the quiet patience of a night owl, having witnessed their entire exchange.

~

TECHMAN EDSEL WINFORD

CHAPTER 9

At first, Edsel didn't give Calvin a reason to regret saving his life. But after the first week of flight simulator sessions, Calvin found one.

The painter hadn't done any lasting damage to his arms, that much was true, yet Calvin was still healing, and the act of tightening his grip sent bursts of hot pain up his forearms, causing the worst of his wounds to ooze. Brian still tried as hard as ever to buck Calvin off of the sawhorse, and much to Calvin's dismay, he pulled it off more than once. Calvin didn't dare ask for mercy either, out of fear that Brian might suddenly remember that he owed Calvin a proper punishment for beating on him last week.

That still had him confused: Brian had caught Calvin under a tarp with Amelia, an association that the Commodore seemed particularly against, yet not a peep. What was the deal?

Calvin pushed it out of his head, reminding himself that he still had to beat Edsel at the simulator. So he kept going, training through the pain, resting as much as possible so he could heal quicker. He regained his strength by the week's end, at the price of having racked up a larger amount of negative tallies by his name than he would have liked. For a while he'd been first on Commodore McCracken's leader board, but he'd surrendered that lead in the wake of the painter attack. Calvin knew that he was better than Edsel, and could prove it if not for his wounds.

By the weekend, Peter and Brian announced another raid on a different British farm. It went easier than Calvin's first raid, and the haul was bigger. He teamed with Peter, raiding some barns and smoke houses while Brian and the others kept the mages occupied. Avery, Cohen and Edsel raided a barn full of grains and corn, but Calvin went for the more valuable stuff: the smoked and cured meats next door. He stumbled out of the brick building with six long chains of smoked sausages hung about him, two large racks of beef ribs, and four cured pork legs. Edsel regarded him with wide-eyed astonishment when he dumped it all in the handcart.

Back at Mount Vernon, Peter congratulated them, giving them earnest praise for their improvement. Calvin personally handed Peter one of the good smoked sausages.

THE FLIGHT SIMULATOR

Peter accepted it but said nothing, fixing Calvin with a smile that hid something he couldn't identify.

Then Commodore McCracken appeared and pulled Peter aside for a private conference, leaving Brian in charge of making sure the raided goods ended up in the pantry. Calvin felt Brian's eyes on him as he worked alongside Stitch and Rusty, shelving cans of grains.

Still no punishment.

*

When they finished, Peter led the cadets out to the dormitory.

"Father wishes to inform you that you have all passed your initial training into the technomancer army. Take a brief moment to feel good about that," he said, looking around the room. Handshakes were exchanged, backs were slapped, and hoots of elation bounced around the small space. Stitch wrapped a big arm around Calvin's shoulders and shook him excitedly. Calvin just waited for the next part of Peter's announcement, which hung in the air like a bubble about to burst.

"I do have some bad news, though. Our messenger, the man Jack Badgett, has passed away. We were able to keep him alive for several days past the curse's normal span, but there was no permanent solution short of actual magic that could have saved him. A study of his body revealed that his collar was not properly buttoned, leaving his neck exposed when he was riding, and that was where the curse hit him. His jacket was treated with powder of frosted iron, yet this one vulnerability did him in. Badgett was unmatched in the air and irreplaceable to the TechMan army. Remember: this can happen to you.

"Even so, his final mission was a success. He brought us valuable intelligence and logistics reports. As it turns out, more soldiers are needed sooner than we thought, so it's a good thing you're ready. The loss of Badgett also means that a new spot is open in the active mimic brigades. One of you will be flying out on Jack's mimic ahead of schedule. Ladies, gentlemen, be ready for anything. The Commodore will make the final announcements tomorrow morning."

Peter departed. The mood shifted in the dormitory, as all eyes settled on Calvin and Edsel.

"It's going to be you," Cohen said to Edsel. "It has to be."

"Right! Calvin rides better and you know it," Stitch said.

"Calvin got too many demerits this week on the simulator," Lyla pointed out.

"Yeah, and they still haven't punished him for attacking Brian," Cohen said.

"He didn't start that fight, he just finished it," Rusty said.

Calvin tuned them out. He looked across the grounds to the stables, where Jack Badgett's mimic stood under a tarp. Amelia walked out of the stables with a bucket in each hand. Her eyes gravitated up and met his stare across the distance. She smiled. He waved at her, and she kept walking toward the house. Noticing movement in the window above the second floor, Calvin saw the unmistakable profile of Commodore McCracken, staring back at him. Pursing his lips, Calvin quietly retreated back into the dormitory.

*

The next morning, they played with guns.

"Final round. Not surprised," Peter said, looking up at the contestants. Calvin and Edsel stood at a bench in the stables, with three firearms in front of either of them, each weapon broken down to its component parts. The competition had begun with sixteen recruits, including the adults, and was now down to just two, though one of the adult cadets had almost edged out Calvin in the last round. Edsel had beaten everyone else handily, including Stitch, who had the highest aggregate score up to that point.

"What's the task?" Edsel asked.

Peter walked them through it. "Assemble the blunderbuss, the rifle, and the pistol, in that order. The pieces are mixed up. So is the ammunition. You must have each weapon affixed to your person, easily accessible and ready for action when you finish. First to finish wins the competition. Brian will judge,"

As Brian stepped up to the bench, Edsel leaned in. "I've so got you."

"Just remember those turkeys," Calvin replied.

"Go," Brian called.

Calvin's hands flew over the equipment, sorting out pieces and brushing aside the ones he didn't need. The steps flew through his mind as he checked them off: the hardened steel funnel of the blunderbuss screwed into the two-piece stock, attach the hinges, lock it all down, pack in a charge, a load of pellets, stuff it in tight, close the hinge, *done*. Calvin buckled the strap and slung it across his torso, the barrel pointed skyward to keep the ammo cluster tight in the chamber.

Edsel matched his every move. Breathing fast, Calvin threw the rifle together, leveling the sight to a preset he'd decided earlier. The bullet casings were all the same color for this exercise, but his discriminating eye picked out the longer shells and dropped them into a cylinder, clipped it into place, locked a cap down on the firing pin and then buckled that weapon to a strap. He slung it crossways on his torso in the opposite direction from the blunderbuss. The butt of his rifle bumped Edsel's, which he also had just slipped over his head.

"Come on, Calvin! You're right on him!"

"Take him, Ed! Faster, faster!"

Their fellow cadets hopped up and down, beckoning them to gain the upper hand. Calvin screwed on the pistol barrel, clicked the hammer assembly into place, and speed-loaded a cylinder, dropping the whole thing into the gun and spinning it once to confirm it would rotate. One shell refused to drop completely, and the half-second he needed to clear it was all the advantage Edsel needed. As he clicked the cylinder shut, half of the young cadets went wild, and the other half booed. The adults mostly chuckled, applauding. Edsel holstered his pistol with a defiant "Ha!" and clapped his hands.

Calvin didn't even blink. Rather than holster his gun, he point-

-ed it at Edsel's head, too close to miss.

The stables went stone silent.

Then Brian burst out laughing.

"Point, Adler. You win."

Edsel flipped. "What? No! That's ridiculous, I met the terms of the challenge!"

"Easily accessible, ready for action? What greater access does he need to a weapon that is already in his hand? How much readier could he be, when it is trained on his target and he can't miss?" Brian asked.

EASILY ACCESSIBLE, READY FOR ACTION...

"But ...mine was ready," Edsel whimpered.

"Then why didn't you use it?" Brian said.

Peter chuckled, arms folded as he leaned against the wall. "Let this be a lesson to you all. The best weapon is the one you already have and can readily use."

Commodore McCracken cleared his throat and entered the stables, leaning on his cane. Everyone snapped to attention, and Calvin fell in line with the others, holstering his pistol. Commodore McCracken looked him up and down, then surveyed Edsel. Without any fanfare, he made his announcement.

"Edsel, you're up first. Get familiar with your mimic; at sundown you're headed to the Ohio." Commodore McCracken gave Calvin a final parting glance, then departed as smoothly as he'd arrived.

Calvin had to retreat a few steps from the rush of recruits that gathered around Edsel, swatting him on the back and telling him good work. Stitch and Rusty hesitated, looking to Calvin as if for approval, but he just shrugged. Stitch and Rusty shook hands with Edsel, who looked like he had just found a chest of buried treasure in his backyard.

Maybe Lyla was right. Maybe my injuries affected me in the simulator, and he scored higher. In a cruel twist of fate, the pain had finally gone the previous night. Calvin flexed his fingers; the muscles in his forearms gave no protest. As much as he wanted something to blame, he couldn't be upset about the painter clawing him up because it had led to Amelia kissing him. Still ...

"Well done," Calvin said, shaking Edsel's hand as he walked by.

"Hey, you too," Edsel beamed. "Next time, yeah?"

"For sure."

Edsel made another round through the excited recruits. Calvin quietly unstrapped his guns, drew his frosted iron knife, and went to work on a dummy in the corner, honing his moves.

~

TECHMAN CALVIN ADLER

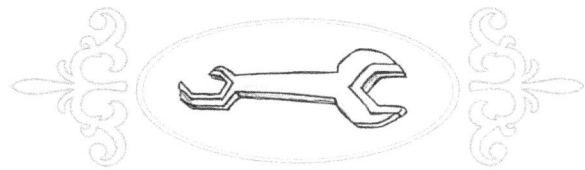

CHAPTER 10

It wasn't Amelia who put a hand over his mouth, but a different McCracken this time.

"Adler. Get up."

Something sharp jabbed him in the ribs. In the faint light penetrating the dormitory entrance he made out the features of Brian's face. Brian lowered his lips to Calvin's ear and whispered, "Pack fast, don't wake the others. Commodore's orders."

Gut burning with sudden anticipation, Calvin reached under his cot and grabbed his pack. Like with his clothing, he'd learned to keep it ready at night. Rubbing the sleep from his eyes, he slung the strap over his shoulder, rose shakily to his feet and followed Brian to the stables. Peter was there with a lantern lit, standing next to Jack Badgett's recently repaired mimic.

"What's this?" Calvin frowned.

"Your new assignment," said Peter.

Calvin wasn't sure he was awake. "But ...Edsel?"

Peter sighed. "Came down with the damned malpox. He's still vomiting blood, we had to quarantine him."

"Whoa!" Calvin exclaimed, earning him a sharp rebuke from Brian's elbow.

"Keep it down!"

"But if he caught it, won't the rest of us?" Calvin asked, rubbing his ribs.

"We don't know. He might have been exposed to it a while ago—a virus can lay dormant for years before flaring up. We'll just have to watch the others. For now you're healthy, so Father assigned you to take his charge," Peter said. He handed Calvin a sealed metal canister with a thin leather strap. "The contents of this are extremely time-sensitive. Our outpost in Youngstown needs it before the weekend."

Hand still trembling, Calvin took the cylinder, turning it over in the dim light. The metal had a frosted iron coating, so it couldn't be magicked away from him.

"That dial on the end has a combination that only Major Tyler knows, at Camp Liberty," Brian said. "If anyone tries to open it in any other way, a chemical bath inside will soak the documents and destroy the contents. Don't let it get to that point."

"Absolutely." Calvin strapped the canister on. He couldn't believe his luck, though he felt bad for Edsel. "What about the rest of my training? I haven't officially finished, have I?"

"These aren't your actual deployment orders, Adler. You're just the only one we can spare. You'll come back from Youngstown when you've delivered this to Major Tyler. Then you'll take your exit exams," Peter said, pushing the mimic's key into Calvin's hand.

Too excited to utter another word, Calvin mounted the mimic, turned it on, and felt the tiny engine thrum between his knees. The lifter fans kicked on, the mimic hovered, and he pulled the lever to retract the landing legs. Slowly rotating a hundred and eighty degrees, he saluted the McCracken brothers and floated out of the stables into the open night. He took one last look at the mansion, wishing he had a chance to say goodbye to Amelia. He would see her when he came back, though.

*

Brian and Peter watched him go, exchanging a wry smile. Wordlessly they returned to the house.

*

Calvin flew like the wind.

Moving at high speeds made the sky cold, and it bit at his exposed flesh. He fished his gloves from his pack as he flew straight over the highest trees, then strapped on his flight goggles to make good use of his eyes. The thrill of flight! Oh, how the simulator failed to do it justice, with the way everything shrank as

THE THRILL OF FLIGHT!

he rose up, and blurred as it sped beneath him. On the sawhorse, he'd held himself up using the handlebars, but up here the wind pushed against him so hard that he pulled on the controls to stay aboard. Before long he found himself pressed down against the fuel tank so as to keep his face behind the small glass windscreen, and this greatly cut down on drag.

This alone was worth joining the army.

He flew for fifteen minutes before a mechanical malfunction changed his fortunes. Without warning the mimic bucked, and a loud *crack* echoed across the night. The engine, which had been somewhat stealthy, now rumbled and groaned, punctuated with a repetitive bark as the motor cycled. Instantly he lost speed, and the wind-drag decreased. Sluggish and loud were two things that he did *not* want to be out here.

Calvin gnashed his teeth and dropped down into a sparse clearing of trees to see what could be done, mentally going through the landing motions like he'd done in the simulator. The mimic's legs touched solid ground and he immediately dismounted, running through another checklist from Horace Whitney's mechanical lectures.

Speed, noise, engine power. What would compromise all three of those?

The muffler.

Thankfully the TechMan engineers had found a way to temper the glass in his goggles so as to allow better vision at night. It wasn't perfect, but he wasn't blind. Calvin dropped to his knees and craned his neck to see beneath the seat. Sure enough, one of the elongated metal cans had ripped open along the weld. He had no desire to roar over the wilderness, drawing the attention of British and French mages, Indian sorcerers, wild beasts and worse. He *had* to fix it.

Nothing in his satchel would solve the problem—he had only weapons, not tools. He remembered Stitch saying something about a compartment under the saddle, and he searched for a way to open it. A button on the tail caused the seat to pop up and flip forward. Inside the compartment, Calvin found a small set of screwdrivers and sockets and a roll of something slick and silvery—a kind of adhesive tape fortified by fiber threads. The stuff was strong, though it smelled a little pungent.

He pushed the two halves of the muffler together and wrapped it with the tape. Aside from smelling, it also made a loud quacking noise when he pulled a strip free from the roll. If the muffler didn't rat him out, this tape would!

Shaking his head, he finished the job, threw the roll back under the seat and fired up the motor. Better. Not as loud, and he'd gotten some of the power back.

He had just risen above the tree level when a mirror on his handlebars showed three silhouetted figures coming up on his tail: one mage on a flying carpet, and two on broomsticks. A night watch! Blast, but those mages were everywhere!

Damn it all!

Calvin opened up the throttle and raced into the night. As

soon as he dared, he reached around and loosed the blunderbuss, assembled and loaded, from his pack. He strung the strap across his torso and fished around in his pack for his pistol. He didn't have the hostler buckled to his waist, but the mimic's saddle had one built in, and he stuffed the loaded weapon into it. It was the best he could do while still flying at full burn.

Another glance in the mirror confirmed that the mages were keeping pace. His heart pounded against his ribs. Blood drummed in his ears, and the night chilled his sweating skin even further until he shivered down to his toes. In the back of his mind, he wondered if this was how Jack Badgett had felt right before he bit it.

~

WINSTON FITZNOTTINGHAM & HAMMOND BIRTWISTLE

CHAPTER 11

No instrument on the mimic's dash kept track of distance. One dial told him his airspeed, another his engine speed, and a third his fuel level. This last one ran dangerously low, and yet the mages dogged him late into the night, not gaining, not falling back. Errant curses flew past him, missing his head by inches, and the occasional one bounced off his dusted jacket.

The weather turned ugly. Clouds smothered the moonlight, and even with his tempered night lenses, Calvin was close to blind, yet he could see curses zipping past him, streams of light that transfigured the clouds into menacing shapes. Feral dogs, winding serpents, and poisonous spiders lashed at him as he sped by. Panting, Calvin hunkered down and willed the little machine to go faster somehow.

The mages didn't give up. Calvin was running out of options, time, and fuel. He couldn't turn because they'd gain on him. He couldn't fight them in the air; they'd be more maneuverable, and they outnumbered him. He had to engage them in a place where numbers and agility mattered little. That meant the woods.

Below him, the trees were as thick as weeds in spring. No way could he fly through them, not at any speed. He'd rip the mimic to pieces before he got thirty feet. Even on foot he'd have his work cut out for him. That didn't mean he was completely out of options, though. Slowing the mimic to quarter speed, he dropped down into a patch of trees that looked like it had been damaged by a storm; roughly forty feet off the ground there opened something like a hole in the woods, and he brought the mimic to a stop midair between two tall spruce trees.

Two anchors hung beneath the pegs where his feet rested. Setting the mimic to hover, he released the anchors, pulled out several yards of cable and cast them out to his sides. A flip of a switch on the dash reeled the spools in tightly, and the anchors found purchase on the trees around him. Once it was secured,

Calvin shut off the mimic, pocketed the key, and kicked a rope ladder down to the ground. He tied off one end around his saddle horn and scurried to the forest floor, keeping one eye on the sky. He touched down as the mage trio closed in on his machine.

"Please, let this work," he whispered.

Voices. They were talking. He held his breath and strained to hear.

"Oi! Where'd he go?" asked one of the broom-riders.

"He's skitted off then?" asked the mage on the carpet. "No, he'd not leave this 'ere for the takin'. Little duffer's 'roundabout somewhere!"

Those voices! Calvin had to cover his own mouth to keep from making a sound. He couldn't believe it. After three weeks and so many miles from home ...he knew these mages. He'd know them anywhere.

Fitznottingham, Birtwistle, and their apprentice.

A special flavor of hatred churned in his gut. This whole mess he was in had started with them; of course it would finish that way. He gripped the strap on his chest, drawing on the proximity of his blunderbuss for reassurance. In the dark, he waited.

"*Leoht!*" Fitznottingham stabbed at the shadows with his wand, and little red flares spat from the tip like fireflies. The flares raced through the trees and cast everything in a haunting light, but the mages must not have seen him. They kept dropping lower, scanning the area.

160

"He's scampered!" Birtwistle said, his words slurred. Hell, even now he was drunk.

Fitznottingham groaned, equally sauced. "Not a chance, Stay here, I'll use a terramancy equation. Let the dirt snitch on the little tosser."

Calvin's neck tingled, the fine hairs bristling in fear. Something was familiar about those words. What had Rusty said? If a mage used one of those equations, they could see beyond the limits of their own senses. That must have been the strange light-spell Fitz had cast over his farm prior to lifting the family savings from their strong box. That was how he'd known where to aim his summoning spell.

The moment Fitz casted that equation, he'd know *exactly* where Calvin was.

But Stitch had a solution for that, Calvin thought. He bit his lip and formed a hastily devised plan.

Winston Fitznottingham stepped off of his fine woolen carpet. Calvin held his breath as he watched the mage move away from Birty and the apprentice. When Calvin judged the distance to be right, he retrieved a clay pot grenade from his satchel, sparked the fuse, and hurled it at the two broom-riders hovering some five feet overhead. Then he squeezed his eyes tight, covered his ears, and ducked behind a stout tree.

The grenade went off, and thudded in the night with a deep, concussive blast. Calvin still flinched despite himself, and his ears rang almost as though his hands hadn't been there. In the closeness of the dense wood, it might as well have been five grenades. But what hurt him would hurt the mages even worse. Calvin unstrapped the blunderbuss and stepped out to survey the damage.

Both wizards had been un-broomed by the blast. The apprentice's legs stuck out from the underbrush, twitching about,

THE GRENADE WENT OFF...

and Birtwistle lay face down in the decaying foliage, unmoving. His broom hung in a high branch above him, its shaft broken in the middle.

Calvin lingered too long in observing his handiwork; from behind him a curse hurtled through the trees and struck his dusted jacket, shattering on contact and shoving him down. A drunken Fitznottingham crashed toward him on foot, wand out, spouting curses in Saxon, most of which kept Calvin off-balance. His first instinct was to go for the pistol, but he'd left it in the saddle overhead. The rifle was too long to use in these trees, and besides, it was still in pieces in his pack.

You idiot! He still had the blunderbuss in hand. He brought it up to bear, but then Fitz's red light spells converged and rushed Calvin's eyes in an attempt to blind him. The tempered goggles didn't darken in time; Calvin closed his eyes and blindly rolled forward, coming to his feet again on Fitz's right. If Fitz had been sober, Calvin had no doubt that he would be dead, or ensnared, or transfigured into a woodland vermin.

But Fitz wasn't sober, and Calvin wasn't helpless. Opening his eyes, he let out a mighty roar and raised the blunderbuss over his head. Fitz tried to do something with his wand, but Calvin brought the butt of the weapon crashing down on Fitz's skull. Fitz cried out and staggered back, his light spells wavering. In all this, he managed to keep a firm grip on his wand, though he didn't point it at Calvin. He raised the tip and summoned more light, enough to bring daylight to the pitch black wood.

"Hammond! Godfrey!" Fitz gnashed his teeth and pressed a palm to a red welt on his forehead. Calvin stepped back and cradled the blunderbuss against his right side, finger on the trigger.

"They're done, Fitz," he said.

Forgetting his pain for a moment, Winston Fitznottingham studied Calvin's face, confused.

"How do you know my name?"

Calvin's heart raced, pumping fire through his veins. This was it. This was the moment John Penn had promised him weeks ago. He'd left his home, left his family behind, for a single shot at standing toe to toe with the mage that had accosted them for years. Here he was, realizing his dream, and Fitz didn't remember him.

He had a moment to fix that.

Calvin raised a hand to his head and palmed the leather cap that covered his hair. He hooked his thumb under his goggles, and in one smooth motion, swept it all off. Fitz's eyes grew wide.

"You're that Adler child! You ran away!"

"And here I am. This one's for Baltimore," Calvin seethed.

He let loose with the blunderbuss. Fitznottingham's final expression would be burned into Calvin's eyes for hours to come. The blast threw Fitz back into the trees. He was dead instantly, and his magical light spells died with him, returning the forest to a realm of shadows, save for dusty streams of moonlight that penetrated the canopy. Calvin could hear nothing over the ringing in his ears. As far as he was concerned, he didn't have to.

The score had been settled.

YOU'RE THAT ADLER CHILD!

Mechanically he slung the blunderbuss back across his torso. This kill had been easier than his first. He'd known Fitznottingham, known what a piece of crap the man was, and Calvin knew plenty of people who had grief from the wayward mage. Now it was done.

He staggered through the forest back to his mimic. Casting a final glance at Birtwistle and the apprentice—both still as death—Calvin nodded to himself and climbed the rope ladder, breathing easy once he was back in the saddle. There, he ignited the engine, pulled up the anchors and set a course for the nearest known oil refinery, feeling an uncanny calm in the wake of it all.

~

GODFREY NORRINGTON

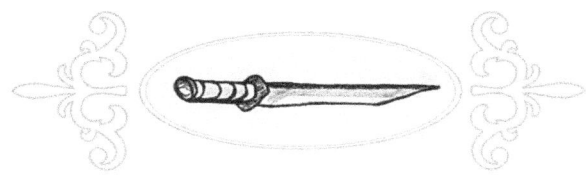

CHAPTER 12

As Godfrey Norrington stirred in the bushes, he became all the more aware that he was painfully far from home.

This had bothered him before, but tonight set a new low standard. He doubted he could get any lower than this, lying on the ground in some unnamed forest in King Charles' empire. Meryka! Of all the places to suffer in exile, they had sent him to the worst hellhole by some distance. Surely Godfrey's crimes did not deserve so savage a punishment.

To boot, they'd placed him under the tutelage of two inept, inebriated gits who failed spectacularly at their jobs—so much so that they'd been demoted from *municipal police duty* to rural perimeter patrol. Word had gotten around to the higher-ups that

Fitz and Birty had sparked a confrontation with the locals, and somebody had stood up to them.

Godfrey had been there on that day. The local—a shepherd's son—hadn't only caused a little mischief, but then too many people had seen him get away with it. The example had caused problems. Baltimore needed ever more surveillance; two mages had died, six more had been assaulted, and by last count, four criminal duffers were still at large. Fitz and Birty were reassigned, to be replaced by sturdier mages.

Somehow in their demotion, they'd kept their assignment over Godfrey. It seemed the fates were curious to see just how far Godfrey could fall. He wondered how much longer he could go living this way before he decided to swallow a spoonful of arsenic and have done with it all.

Thorny branches pricked at his skin through his shirtsleeves, and Godfrey struggled to disentangle himself from the hostile foliage. Pain took a new bite out of him with every movement. In his heart of hearts, he knew he'd been injured badly. That bright flash, then the loud bang, and his world had spun like an enchanted saucer. His thoughts swam through a thick, ethereal ooze in his throbbing head, trailed by disjointed sounds and images. He should really get up. He should check on Fitznottingham and Birtwistle.

He found it arduous to convince his body to move.

Bested by some brat with a toy that went boom.

Brat. Such an ugly word. His own father and mother had used it on him too many times back home in Birmingham. Their faces swirled around him, tormenting him, taunting him for his weakness.

You're a pox on our house, boy, Father had said. *Get comfortable over there in Meryka. You won't be coming back.*

Sir Waldo Norrington talked a lot about what level he was on, but it was a joke. He'd been born no better than anyone else—a near crime in Britain—and worked his way up the social ladder until he'd landed a seat in Parliament, in charge of a subcommittee that oversaw a transatlantic teleportal network. Now he shoveled his portly mass into a wig and robes every morning, looked in a mirror and told himself he was important. Bah. Father represented the weakest district on the island. He pretended not to hear the whispers of his colleagues, believing that if he acted the part long enough, others would buy the farce as well.

This had frustrated Godfrey to the point of acting out just to crack his father's shell. His deeds were petty at first; he'd started by insulting people at Father's parties, then upgraded to vandalism and boisterous outbursts at the theater. These were harmless enough, but when Sir Clive Brimble had stumbled upon Godfrey in a bout of slap-and-tickle with his daughter Hannah—on the desk in Brimble's home study, no less—a line had been crossed. Brimble was Father's chief rival in Parliament, representing a competing faction. Though Godfrey tended to ignore the particulars of governmental proceedings, he knew he'd thrown a bad spell.

Rather than suffer the embarrassment of an uncouth son, Sir Waldo had exiled Godfrey to the Merykan colonies, where he was inducted into the Royal Mage Corps against his will. Perhaps Father had thought that policing the colonials would build character and purge Godfrey's rash behavior. Godfrey had feared as much before coming to Meryka—anything that "built character" was another name for a spectacular waste of time.

He'd always heard that Meryka was a land of deported undesirables, prisoners, and ignorant laborers, but nothing had prepared him for living among their class of people. Shaking them down for extra crowns had been fun while it lasted, before Fitz and Birty had managed to properly bugger that up as well: the Department of Magical Espionage had discovered that the so-called "technomancers" had recruited a dozen people from Baltimore, a crime that might have been prevented if the senior mages had been doing their jobs. Fitz and Birty's dereliction had been their downfall.

Godfrey wasn't made for this. He desired power, command over subjects, and the respect of his peers. He had already learned from his father that being the king of bilge rats still made one a bilge rat. Even if Godfrey were to excel and rise to the top of the Royal Mage Corps, what would it matter?

Sir Waldo would not let Godfrey come home. He oversaw the runework on the long-range teleportation platforms that moved troops and materials from the Isles to the Continent, and no amount of trickery would let Godfrey bypass the security spells. Pleading wouldn't work either. Godfrey needed some kind of amazing haul, something to add prestige to the family name. Unless he could steal a dragon with long-range flight capabilities, he would not see the shores of England any other way.

Until then, he was a fly in a web, stuck in this dark place until it sucked the life out of him.

Pawing around in the darkness, his fingers brushed the shaft of his wand and closed on it. He cast a quick healing spell on his stinging eyes and ears, and the sounds and sights of the forest rushed back into clear relief.

"Ungh!" Godfrey sucked in a wet breath and drew the fastest terramancy equation he could muster, mind racing as he focused on the flood of information that came to him.

That vile colonial boy and his infernal machine were long gone. Godfrey's broom was ruined, as was Birtwistle's. Birty was unconscious, maybe even dead, his body slumped over in the bushes to Godfrey's right. Fitznottingham was ...close? But he wasn't moving, and Godfrey's magic was fouled up by the presence of frosted iron. Had the machinist been carrying that on him?

Clever sod. Godfrey stood and brushed his clothes, wondering if he'd gotten any of the poisonous dust on his robe. Curse that renegade machinist and his...

Godfrey froze.

Renegade machinist.

Bob's your bloody uncle, that would do it!

The reports stated that that the technomancers had a vast, secretive, nigh impenetrable network. Those that had been taken alive soon killed themselves with poison capsules. They were a thorn in the side of the Empire, with the potential to become much worse if they weren't cut down in their infancy. He'd heard that they even raided the Crown's supply farms down south. Tonight marked his first sighting of one, and he'd survived. Was there some way to catch him? Maybe Fitz's carpet was still intact?

"Winston! Hammond!" Godfrey called. The woods swallowed his words, and equally blocked any response that might have come. He cast an illumination spell and stumbled about until he came across Fitz's flying carpet, half-covering a fresh corpse.

Godfrey gasped. The little vermin! He'd killed Winston Fitznottingham, a badged and licensed mage of the Crown! Not only was he a machinist, this boy was a runaway murderer! Godfrey could not believe his luck.

"Catch him," he told himself. "Catch this brat and bring him to justice, and Father will *beg* you to come home. *Secan!*"

Waving his wand about, he cast a searching spell over Fitz. The mage's badge hung inside his robe, against his breast. Godfrey took the badge—it carried more authority than his own—and turned to take the rug. Something tugged at him though, at his mind, prodding him to search again. Frowning, Godfrey raised his wand again and uttered a second spell: *"Ternes!"*

A moment later, a call came back, spoken in colonial English, clear as a bell: *This one's for Baltimore.*

A ghost of the words hung in the heavy forest air, laced with anger and something akin to righteous indignation. Godfrey reached out with his magic and absorbed the essence of them, trying to understand their context, and what had happened as they'd been said. There was a declaration, the feeling of victory, of retribution ...the boy had uttered this just before killing Fitznottingham with a loud and violent weapon.

Godfrey pondered on their meaning, repeating the spell half a dozen times ...why did this sound so familiar? This particular shade of bright red anger called to his mind. Godfrey racked his memory for the answer.

*Yes! I*t was that brat who'd doused Fitz in filthy water, and then punched Birty. *Baltimore.* Godfrey had taken a reading of the boy's emotions at the time; he'd known he was lying. He'd done it on purpose, without his parents' approval...

Godfrey raced to piece it together. The son hated mages, wanted to assault them, the father said no, so the son ran away and joined the technomancers. Whether by fate or fortune, Godfrey had crossed paths with the angry duffer. He knew what opportunity looked like, and he would not let it escape his grasp.

This one's for Baltimore. Such a tense declaration, sealed with a slaying, might as well have been a compass spell. Using his wand, Godfrey drafted a series of complicated runes in the air.

"Gesamnian!"

A hazy cloud lit up around him, the dregs of the boy's red-hot anger. Godfrey finished his incantation with a flourish and ushered the haze into an empty potion vial. He stowed the hardened glass bottle in a sash at his waist. Protocol dictated that he find the nearest mage precinct and file a report. Sod that. He would bag this prey himself.

With Fitz's badge in hand, Godfrey stepped onto the carpet and ascended out of the thick woods. The bottled spell pointed straight and true, guiding him with deadly precision.

To his next encounter with the Boy from Baltimore.

And this time, the result would be very different.

SOD THE PROTOCOL.

~

CAPTAIN EUSTICE HAMILTON

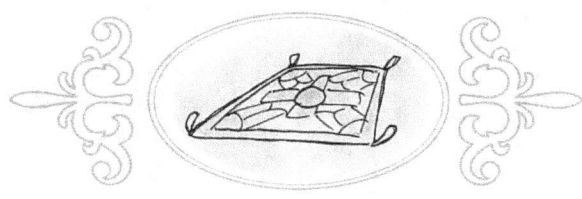

CHAPTER 13

In the back of his mind Calvin heard one of the McCrackens say something about flying in broad daylight: you weren't supposed to do it. Calvin's anxiety outpaced his exhaustion, and he pushed himself to the limit. Half an hour after he escaped the mages, he came across a petroleum refinery that Peter and Brian had marked on a map, and Calvin managed to steal eight gallons of kerosene to power the mimic. Then he flew well past sunrise.

At dawn he dipped low and accidentally buzzed an Iroquois village hidden in the woods. Some of them had magic—different from the British mages but still as potent—and they lobbed arrows at him over supernaturally long distances. He escaped without further incident, flying until high noon, when he shut down on the peak of a mountain and collapsed over the hump of the mimic's fuel tank, falling asleep instantly.

For many hours, he slept.

*

He woke up, stiff and aching, with a dull protest in his chest from the fuel cap. He twisted from side to side to pop his spine, which had tightened up like an overdried leather braid. When he dismounted to relieve himself, two sharp pinpricks in his back notified him that he had in fact been shot by the Iroquois. Frowning, he slipped the coat off and found two arrows and a tomahawk embedded in the thick material.

"Seriously?" he muttered. To the jacket's credit, he hadn't even felt them hit. The frosted iron had done its job. Calvin plucked out the weapons and dropped them on the ground, thought better of it, and put them in his satchel. Better not to leave extra evidence that he'd been here.

The sun dipped lower to the horizon, bathing the western sky in a rich, reddish-orange light. Calvin shrugged back into the jacket but left it unbuttoned in the front, and likewise only strung his goggles on around his head. His thoughts kept drifting back to Fitz, and how he'd killed a man for the second time.

He didn't relish the feeling. As much as he hated Fitz and Birty, he would have preferred if they'd just up and left. But if he hadn't finished the fight, he knew they'd have come back with worse. All he could think of was that afternoon in Tanner's yard, when he'd worked up the guts to grab that bucket and take action.

"There's nothing pretty about this," he said aloud, as if lecturing himself. "I know that now. It's this, or we keep living the way we always have." Calvin looked down at his gloved hands, studying the worn leather across his palms. "*You can do any job with the right tool.* Even a dirty job."

He chewed on his own words. Maybe it would bother him for a while. He could live with that; he couldn't live the rest of his life knowing that he had a chance to be free, and had let it go. Father had chosen that path. Not him.

Contenting himself with this fact, Calvin took one last look at the setting sun before mounting his mimic and resuming his flight. He still had enough fuel to get to Youngstown without stopping.

*

He made it by midnight. What he saw scared him.

From the sky he could see where the city had begun, near the black foothills rich with coal. The buildings changed in style the farther they moved out, like layers of an onion, their architecture having altered as the city expanded over time. At one point the place had been large, maybe even as big as Baltimore, until some terrible calamity had befallen it. Now it was a ghost town.

The moon waxed larger tonight, and without the canopy of so many trees Calvin could see much better than he had in the woods the night before. Pale blue light cast shadows on the city, and the scene smelled of ash. Buildings stood half-destroyed in a pile of bricks, their inner pylons toppled over. Roads buckled up, burnt trees stood leafless along the walkways, and not a single glass window remained intact.

What had happened here? Well, other than the mages finding the place, that is. In some spots, objects had been transfigured; stone barricades were partially converted to flower petals, or wooden shops and buildings had been reduced to piles of sand and sawdust. Behind the barricades stood discarded cannons and ankle-deep piles of spent bullet casings.

There had been an all-out fight here. Man against mage, no holding back. And the army had clearly lost.

Calvin's heart fluttered. Youngstown had been leveled! Should he go back to Mount Vernon? Maybe between the time Jack Badgett got his intelligence and the time the McCrackens dispatched Calvin, the mages had swarmed the technomancers' outpost ...but no. The longer Calvin searched the rubble, hovering silently down the broken roads, the more he started to think that this damage took place a while ago. Maybe even years. The few bodies that he saw—he tried not to throw up—had decayed too much for a recent battle.

At the next intersection he turned right. A larger building stood in the center of the square, with pillars holding up a domed roof. The half-burned sign on the lawn proclaimed it to be the justice building at City Hall. The steps were clear of debris, and Calvin thought it a good place to stop and unclog the lifter fans, which had sucked up a lot of ash in the last ten minutes. He had only just flown up the main walkway when a massive pile of debris shifted on the overgrown lawn, bowled aside as though pushed by a massive hand from below, revealing a wide, dark hole that went deep underground. Two great shadows emerged from the hole, and in the weak light of his ash-covered headlamps he made out the faint silhouettes of two gryphons.

"Nope!" Calvin jerked the handlebars to the side and revved the throttle.

He sped over the grass, fighting for altitude. The lifter fans squealed in protest. Forced to stay low, he went to the end of the block and cut left, hoping the headlights would warn him of any obstacles.

He needn't have worried; brighter lights shown down on him from behind. The noise of larger engines assaulted his ears. He felt a presence zoom overhead, reach the end of the street and drop to his level, pointing a pair of blindingly bright headlights at him. Calvin averted his eyes and wrenched his air flaps open to bring his mimic to a halt, thumb hovering over the triggers to the two belly guns underneath.

Then he realized his mistake: these were mimics, not actual gryphons.

An amplified voice boomed through the glare. *"State your purpose!"*

Calvin squinted hard. "I'm a technomancer!"

"What is your base of origin?"

"I'm out of Mount Vernon!" He held up the canister, still strapped across his chest.

MIMICS, NOT ACTUAL GRYPHONS...

The lights went out. Calvin blinked several times to adjust to the darkness again, and he saw the profile of a gryphon mimic, complete with pilot and gunner. The gunner, dressed from head to toe in some type of plate armor, fast-roped off the back of the gryphon and deftly maneuvered through the debris in the road to examine Calvin's canister. "I have to give it to Major Tyler," Calvin said, hoping he sounded official enough. "McCracken's orders."

"You're cleared. Follow our six back into the tunnel," the gunner said, pointing at City Hall. Calvin didn't know what a six was, so he just stayed between the two gryphons.

So. There were still technomancers in Youngstown.

*

The rubble on the lawn was part of a huge hydraulic device that covered a secret door into the technomancers' underground hideout which, Calvin soon saw, was even larger than the city above. Supported by thick stone pillars, the base spread out for what looked like a mile, bustling with activity even at this hour.

He steered the dragonling straight down a forty-foot shaft into an open landing pit with a fifty-foot ceiling. Spread out below him was an entire fleet of mimics in a variety of models, parked in neat lines, and the farther he dropped, the more came into view. The base had multiple floors and levels, like a giant bowl-shaped stadium that eventually led to an open space some two hundred feet beneath the surface.

Wherever anyone was working or standing by, they used electric lanterns and gaslight to provide illumination. Parts of the ground were paved where necessary, but by and large the floor was mostly level dirt and gravel.

Something like this has been here for a long time, and I hadn't the slightest idea.

The gryphons flanked him during the descent, then broke off and told him to follow. Calvin stayed on their tails until they arrived at the far edge of the motor pool, where they landed and disembarked. He followed the gryphons to a huge area full of other mimics, separated by size and model. Calvin found an empty spot among the dragonlings, and his escorts parked their machines with the gryphons. One of the pilots approached him and removed his helmet. Calvin recognized him right away.

"John Penn?"

"In the flesh, kid. Three weeks into training and they gave you a mimic?"

"Yeah ...it wasn't supposed to be me, but another guy got sick. Actually it wasn't supposed to be him on this thing either," Calvin said, brushing ash off of his sleeves.

John eyed the saddle and gasped. "Jack Badgett! What happened?"

Calvin presented the cylinder. "That's why I'm here."

"But, Mount Vernon! Is everything okay there?"

"It was when I left."

John nodded. He wanted to ask more, but he seemed like he had somewhere to be. "Come on. I'll take you to the Major."

They left the motor pool, following a colored footpath along one wall. This led to a section of the undercity that had been turned into offices and laboratories for higher-ranking TechMan officers. Calvin peered through some windows as they walked.

"What happened to the city up there? And how did you guys dig this place out?" he asked John.

"Youngstown has been like this for a hundred years. Used to be a coal mine, filled with slaves and prisoners. All of them were duffers, of course," John said with a hint of bitterness. "They strip-mined the whole place and couldn't go any deeper without seriously buggering the stability on the surface. After that, the King turned it into a political prison. This was where he hid the people he really hated, the ones who caused him the most trouble. People like the first technomancers."

"But you freed them?" Calvin asked.

"Not me personally, no. Maybe ten years back, some earlier technomancers gave it a try. It didn't go so well. They took control of the prison, but then the mages laid siege to the city. Our side had access to huge stocks of iron-based metals that they weren't willing to surrender—too many weapons and machines could be made from it all. But they couldn't break the siege either, so they organized a false retreat down into the mines and let the King's forces think they'd suffocated. Burn the topside to ash, pump some frosted iron dust up through the ventilation system, and boom: you've got a fortress that they won't invade unless they have to," John said.

"Damn," Calvin breathed, finding a newfound appreciation for the expansive space.

"Yeah. This place is one of our best-kept secrets. A lot of good men and women died down here. Now, upon their bones we build the vehicles of their justice."

They rounded a corner into a hallway with a low ceiling, lit by gas lanterns. From the other end came a soldier in combat fatigues, sporting a pistol on his hip and a sturdy metal helmet tucked under one arm. His jacket looked like Calvin's, only more worn and decorated with medals for things Calvin could only guess at. John Penn snapped to attention, though the newcomer was a good ten years younger. Calvin decided to salute as well.

"Captain Hamilton," John said.

"At ease, Leftenant. Who's the riffraff?"

"A new TechMan from Mount Vernon. No rank yet, it appears he was sent out before graduation."

"I have a message for Major Tyler," Calvin said.

John stepped in front of Calvin, blocking his view of Captain Hamilton. "My apologies sir, he doesn't yet know protocol."

"McCracken sent us a wet-behind-the-ears greenhorn? That's some crap," Hamilton said with a grunt. Calvin already didn't like this guy, whoever he was.

"The situation sounded dire. Jack Badgett has been taken out," John explained.

Hamilton groaned. "You're relieved of the charge, Leftenant. You! Come with me." He snapped his fingers. John moved aside and pushed Calvin forward.

"Do as he tells you, Adler. And don't speak to an officer without being spoken to first."

His pride wounded, Calvin frowned and followed Captain Hamilton back down the hall to a guarded door. The guards didn't stop Hamilton, though; he walked right through and pulled Calvin in after him.

"Your weapons." Hamilton slapped the top of a metal table on one side of the small room, an antechamber to another room beyond.

Calvin almost protested. Sensing that would be a bad idea, he removed the blunderbuss, the pack with the rifle, and the Iroquois weapons he'd stowed.

"Where's your pistol?"

"Holstered on my mimic," Calvin said.

"It's not your mimic. Keep track of your weapons," Hamilton said.

I know where it is, Calvin wanted to say.

"And what about your knife?"

Sheathed and strapped to my calf, where I can get to it. "Lost it in the woods. I was attacked by three mages." He decided to keep something on him. Hamilton might be a TechMan officer, but Calvin knew a hostile when he saw one.

"It's not like McCracken to unleash an incompetent on the world. I would've made you walk home," Hamilton grumbled. "Inside." He pushed Calvin through the next door.

On the other side was a lush office. The temperature was

comfortable, the smell reminded him of his mom's cooking, and the place was neat and tidy like most of the rooms at Mount Vernon. At the desk in the center of the room sat a woman in a dress uniform. She was hunched over a stack of maps and official-looking documents. Her short gray-blonde hair was pulled into a stub of a tail. Calvin guessed her to be about fifty years old. She had an air about her that suggested he ought not trifle with her.

"Major Tyler, sir, Commodore McCracken sent an unranked recruit with a sealed canister," Hamilton said.

Calvin's eyes went wide. This was Major Sam Tyler?

Tyler didn't look up from her work. She held out a hand for the canister. Hamilton pried it from Calvin and passed it to his superior officer. Tyler examined the number dial, spun in a code and popped off the end of the canister like she'd done it a thousand times. Inside was a rolled-up sheet of paper. She scanned it over, grunted, and tossed it aside.

"That's fine. Set him up with 7MB."

"Sir?" Hamilton asked, sounding just as confused as Calvin.

Tyler looked up, her eyes hard as steel. "He's not unranked. Says right here, he's a TL3. You brought him to me to handle this? You're wasting my time, Captain."

Hamilton stiffened. Calvin took a small bit of enjoyment at his discomfort before proceeding.

"Ma'am," Calvin began.

"*Sir,*" Tyler corrected him. Hamilton bristled at Calvin's breech of conduct, but Tyler waved him off. "Out with it, TechMan."

MAJOR SAMANTHA TYLER

"Sir, if I may ...Commodore McCracken's orders were very clear that I was to hand this to you personally," he said. "It has something to do with Jack Badgett. I'm afraid he's passed away."

"I already know that. Word of Badgett's death came over the airwaves two days ago. Only those in the command chain are aware of it, and you'll keep it that way, TechMan."

The air took on an eerie chill. Calvin's gut twisted.

"But ...they said it was time-sensitive. Sir," he added.

"Must be a mistake, TechMan," Tyler said. She handed the paper to him. Calvin read it as quickly as he could. There wasn't much on it.

It was a draft order, assigning Calvin Adler to Major Sam Tyler's command at Youngstown, Ohio. His signature was at the bottom, in a passable imitation of his own handwriting. He had never signed any such document.

"This can't be right. I was supposed to deliver news to you and then return to Mount Vernon," Calvin said.

"Cold feet are the mark of a coward, TechMan," Hamilton sneered. "You're not going anywhere. A man's word is his bond."

"This isn't supposed to be me!" Calvin thrust the paper at Hamilton. "This is supposed to be Edsel Winford. He got the assignment to come here."

Bored, Major Tyler shuffled through a stack of small notes on the corner of her desk. "No, TechMan Winford reported to Pittsburgh yesterday morning, as per Commodore McCracken's orders. Captain, I don't have time for this, get TechMan Adler over to 7MB. Dismissed."

Calvin's swayed as his heart sank. He didn't have it in him to fight Hamilton, who grabbed him by the arm and dragged him out of the room. Hamilton might have issued more insults to his honor, but it all fell on deaf ears; Calvin's head swam with the realization that he'd been betrayed.

Was this finally the penalty for beating Brian? Or had the Commodore found out about Calvin and Amelia? He was supposed to be headed for Baltimore, and instead they'd relegated him to a distant underground outpost.

A prison.

And he'd walked right into it.

~

TECHNOMANCER HANK DUNCAN

CHAPTER 14

Godfrey stood to stretch his sore legs, then knelt on the carpet and peered over the edge. The ground was about thirty feet below him. In the moonlight, Youngstown, Ohio looked like a three-square-mile heap of ash. He'd heard about this place when Birt got drunk one night and sang "God Save the King" at the top of his lungs. Fitz, equally smashed, had started counting off British military victories on his fingers, all the way back to when the mages had stomped out that uppity rabble-rouser, George Washington. One of the victories he'd listed was more recent: the annihilation of Youngstown, and the humiliation of the technomancer army.

Godfrey spat on the ashes. Technomancers? An offensive

notion. These duffers thought that by employing little metal toys, they would somehow raise themselves to the level of a mancer.

He checked the bottle that contained the boy's emotional imprint. *For Baltimore.* The spell had lost considerable strength over so many miles, and now the reception was fuzzy. Godfrey doubted he'd find anything else here—the spell might even be suffering from interference, from the lingering influence of whatever passion the rabble-rousers had imprinted here during their last stand.

Swearing under his breath, Godfrey tapped his wand on the bottle and muttered a spell of preservation. He had to save what little he had of the boy's imprint. From there, it behooved him to find a sangromancer. Blood magic was not his best discipline, and a skilled blood worker would know better what to do with this sort of thing.

He sat back on the carpet and rode south, wondering where he would find a bloodworker.

*

Hamilton's smug cackling stabbed Calvin like knives in his brain. "Never gets old, seeing you limp-legged new guys come in here all scared and regretful. What, did you think training camp was as hard as it would get?"

Calvin didn't reply. His mind was hundreds of miles away, back at Mount Vernon, aflame with rage at the McCrackens and their treachery. A week ago he would have loved to be in the field, assigned to a mimic and a brigade, surrounded by machines and weapons and fellow technomancer soldiers. Now his whole mind labored to find an escape from this place.

He would make this right.

Amelia ...

He scanned his surroundings, absorbing details at every turn. Hamilton had led him to a row of barracks, each one full of technomancers in fatigues going about their business. A flag hung over every door, indicating that squad's function with a name and number. One flag proudly proclaimed "28th Riflemen Brigade, Lazy Eyes." Another read "19th Infantry Brigade, Dirt Kickers."

Hamilton abruptly pushed Calvin into an open tent on his left. He didn't get a good look at the flag, other than an angry red heart crossed with a star-spangled X. Inside the tent were five cots but only four occupants. He guessed he would be the fifth.

"Duncan, this one's yours. Got a new guy," Hamilton said. Without any ceremony, he spun on his heel and left, chuckling to himself as he went.

Duncan rose to his feet. Calvin figured he was maybe seventeen or eighteen, just a few years older than he was, with dark brown skin and black hair woven in tight rows. Duncan smiled genuinely.

"Hey, what's up? Hank Duncan, Brigade Leader. These are your teammates"

"Calvin Adler. Look Hank, there's been a mistake, I was sent here under a false pretense and I need to get back up to the surface. When do we train outside?" Calvin asked.

Hank and the others laughed, some mirthlessly. They went

196

back to lying on their cots or polishing their boots.

"Happens all the time, man. Not to worry. A lot of us got tricked in, but you'll get past that," Hank said.

"You don't understand, I—"

"I do, really well actually. I just wanted to get trained to fight in New Hampshire, but they sent me here to the border with New France. We keep the French and the Iroquois at bay," Hank said.

"I thought we were fighting the British."

"Them too. There's more than one front to this war. You're still helping the cause, Adler."

"I'm supposed to be somewhere else," Calvin insisted.

"Just take a deep breath, get situated and catch some sleep. What matters is that we hold the line here," Hank said.

Calvin shuffled numbly toward the empty cot. Hank would prove ultimately useless, it seemed. As Calvin sat down and stared at the wooden plank floor, mind spinning, Hank clapped him on the back.

"You're a technomancer now, of the 7th Mimic Brigade. Welcome to the Rebel Hearts."

END BOOK ONE

The fight is not over!

Calvin Adler will ride again, in

ENGINES OF LIBERTY:
SUICIDE RUN

Coming early 2015!

SMACK DOWN GENTLE!

(ACKNOWLEDGMENTS)

There are two kinds of people who read the "thank-you" page: those who think they might be in it, and everyone else. So I've made it easy with underlines and whatnot, to save you time. (And please know that if you're in the latter camp, Jesus still loves you.)

THANK YOUS go to:

<u>Schaara</u>, for her endless support and patience with the real-life neuroses that occur in a marriage when someone is a writer. Thank you for always being there to hold me up. I love you, babe.

<u>Mom,</u> who has been my biggest cheerleader since I got into creative writing twenty years ago, and always thought I could pull it off.

<u>Mamaw</u>, who would wistfully watch as I sketched away the hours of my youth, and made me promise to do something career-wise with my drawing skills. The first drawing that I finished for REBEL HEART would've been on her 78th birthday. Miss you, Mamaw.

<u>Nana,</u> who read some of the really bad sci-fi I wrote in high school, and didn't encourage me to take up a career in accounting instead. Love you, Nana!

<u>Moira</u>, for coming to the rescue when I needed to scan a ton of huge drawings, and every other option sucked. Check out her blog: moirialianephotography.blogspot.com

Jordan, for applying the weight of academic criticism to an otherwise eye-rolling piece of genre fiction. You fixed a great many faults with your suggestions; that Ph.D finally paid off.

Raelene, whose knowledge of fonts and typefaces helped me pick a visual theme for the text.

Shante, who's been tremendously enthusiastic about a number of my unpublished projects, and is a valuable proofreader. You earned that namesake character!

Emily and Holly, the *femmes fatales* at Castle Editorial, who did a bang-up job of telling me every single thing that I did wrong, without saying outright that I suck. *Merci*, ladies!

Savannah Weech, who's probably read even more of my writing than my wife. One of these days I'll get you a decent piece that you can narrate, bud.

Carter Reid, who nailed the cover art, and did a big load of follow-up work to make sure it all came together. (Check out his webcomic, www.thezombienation.com.)

Mark Asper and Nemiha Studebaker, for volunteering their young relatives so that I could steal their faces and put them on small side characters.

Matt Jones, for his fortitude and masculinity. Kings to you.

Thank you to those whose faces landed on certain characters:

Patrick McConaha (Calvin Adler)

Joseph McConaha (Godfrey Norrington)

Megan Hibbert (Amelia McCracken)

Shante McConaha (Shantewa Goodall)

Zachariah Parry (Edsel Winford). *You get credit for sending me pics when I asked for a "smug jerk."*

Bart Gadbury (Captain Hamilton). *You get credit for volunteering to be a psychopath with a "punchable face."*

Allie Martin (Lyla)

Jimmy Martin (Stitch)

Kara Martin (Rusty)

Jedi Damery (Cohen)

Cameron Hale (Avery)

James A. Owen (Winston Fitznottingham)

J. Scott Savage (Hammond Birtwistle)

Pretty much everyone else was modeled after a celebrity or athlete or something, and they're already famous enough, so bah.

Other professional gratitude is extended to:

The Eagle Mountain Writers: Debbie, DJ, Donna, Linda, Kirk, Ryan, and Arlene. (The only writing group in the galaxy to have completed the Kessel Run in twelve parsecs!) But really, the way you've built me up and brought me in over the years has meant so much. Keep writing.

James A. Owen: First off, thanks for writing all the great fiction that you've put out there. More so, thanks for writing the highly inspirational DRAWING OUT THE DRAGONS. It is responsible for this book in no small part. And above all, thanks for joining our writing group for dinner at LTUE in 2012. That was a complete Over Nine Thousand fanboy moment for me. You're the man. Naturally the only way to truly express my admiration was to have you get blown away by a fifteen year-old with a steampunk shotgun in the woods somewhere. (Whoops, spoiler.)

J. Scott Savage: In 2009 you gave a classy response to a rather unclassy review of your YA fantasy series *FarWorld*. I believe the culprit was some Internet turd who went by the handle "GrahamChops." I've learned a great deal about professionalism from you in the intervening years, and I thank you for keeping your cool in a situation where I most assuredly may not have. For what it's worth, your character didn't die in this book, but he will in the sequel.

A.J. Paquette: You're a good friend, a great writer, and you were a fantastic agent for those two years. I can't overstate your influence on my writing, and I thank you for all of the unrewarded hours that you poured into at least three, and technically four, of my unpublished books. I wish you every success.

A blanket thanks goes to all the writers of my childhood, a period which by most metrics has not really ended.

And finally, thank you to all of the heroes, unsung and otherwise, who fought in the War of Independence those centuries ago. Because of you, there's a land today where I can make my dreams real. We're forever in your debt.

About the Author

Graham Bradley began writing at the age of 8, and it's been a bad habit ever since. He enjoys cars, history, the Indianapolis Colts, BBQ, reading, and traveling. He currently lives in Henderson, Nevada, with his wife and son.

REBEL HEART is his first published book.

(Thank you for reading.)

Twitter.com/GrahamBeRad

Instagram.com/GrahamBeRad